CHAIN OF CUSTODY

CHAIN OF CUSTODY

Scott I. Zucker

authorHOUSE®

AuthorHouse™
1663 Liberty Drive
Bloomington, IN 47403
www.authorhouse.com
Phone: 1-800-839-8640

First published by AuthorHouse   01/04/2012

ISBN: 978-1-4685-3162-6 (sc)
ISBN: 978-1-4685-3161-9 (ebk)

Printed in the United States of America

CHAPTER 1

"Good afternoon, your Honor, I am Matthew Taggart, counsel for Jamison Pharmaceuticals."

"Yes, Mr. Taggart, come on in." The elderly black robed judge responded.

Taggart walked cautiously into the large oak paneled chambers of senior federal court Judge Jonathan H. Lantham. "Of course you know Mr. Davidson, counsel for the Plaintiffs." The Judge gestured to the man already sitting in one of the large leather chairs situated in front of the Judge's large mahogany desk.

"Yes sir," Taggart reached out his hand to the other lawyer, who rose slightly off his chair, shook hands obligingly and then sat back down. Taggart found the other chair in front of the Judge's desk, sat down in the worn leather seat and opened his briefcase, removing a notepad.

"I called you both in here to resolve the discovery dispute you seem to be having in the case," the Judge started out, his eyes now peering over the papers he was reading as he reclined in his chair. "I want all these motions to end and I want to see some progress on this case. This matter has been sitting on my docket for over a year now, and you both are still in discovery. You either settle this case or I'm setting a trial date whether or not you finish discovery."

Judge Lantham had laid down the law. Not surprisingly, since that was his reputation, to be tough, but fair. He either forced disputing parties to settle their cases or made sure that they were ready to try them. In this case, since millions of dollars were at stake, he knew he had to push the parties along or that the case would continue to be bogged down in lawyers' busy work of motions pleading. Taggart already knew what he was in for before he'd even walked into the Judge's chambers. The Judge's clerk, or "staff attorney" as was the politically correct title, had explained the Judge's purpose for the Monday morning meeting when the in-chambers conference had been scheduled, but he wasn't ready for the other shoe to drop.

"And Mr. Taggart, with reference to Mr. Davidson's motion to compel concerning his document requests, I will tell you now that I'm inclined to rule in the Plaintiffs' favor on this one. Jamison has failed to give one credible reason why it has not produced its research records on this drug, what's it called . . . Tribucal. This is the central issue that you're fighting over. I'll give you two weeks to respond. If you don't give me some good reason why the documents haven't been produced, I'll grant the order."

"What about the Plaintiffs' request for attorneys' fees, your honor?" Davidson asked.

"We'll take that up in two weeks," the Judge responded.

"Your Honor," Taggart interrupted, "we're dealing with significant issues of company trade secrets and proprietary information. Jamison can't turn that information over until the Plaintiffs meets their *prima facie* case for even alleging that this drug caused the death. Otherwise, it's just an open door to Jamison's medical technology. Judge, they're asking for too much."

"Your Honor, we can't prove our case until we see their research notes to verify that they misrepresented the results of their clinical tests," Davidson rebutted.

"Gentlemen, work it out, or I will. I suggest you consider some confidentiality agreement or some other way to get this done. I'm due back on the bench." The Judge got up from behind his desk and started walking toward the doorway in his office that led back to the courtroom.

The two lawyers rose and began gathering their papers. Taggart thought to himself that even though it had gone poorly that at least it had been mercifully quick. He also wondered how he was going to have time to work on the response to the motion on top of the other assignments waiting for him that were lined up on his desk. He was kind of in a fog as he packed up his briefcase and began walking out the Judge's chambers.

As they left the outer office, Davidson held the door for Taggart and remarked how awful the Orioles game had been the night before "we need better pitching, don't ya' think Matt?" Davidson had that sort of guy next door, neighborly approach. It worked well with juries. Matt nodded. "It would help too if they could hit the ball," Davidson added with a laugh.

Matt realized that Davidson, a twenty-five year veteran of personal injury law, was not going to be an easy adversary, quite the opposite. Matt figured that Davidson probably had all of his experts lined up to crucify Jamison, plus he had the husband of this lady who died, her three children and two small grandchildren. They were good people. They made for better Plaintiffs.

The two lawyers traveled down the elevator together to the first floor. Davidson asked which way Matt was going and Matt told him that he had to go to the Clerk's office, simply to avoid having to endure a continuation to their conversation. As Davidson turned to leave toward the building exit he commented to Matt "you really ought to meet my clients. All they're looking for are answers. Women like Iris Forslin don't die at 53. You really ought to meet them."

"I guess I will, at least at the depositions." Matt replied.

"Yes, Yes," Davidson said. "We'll have to start planning those. I'll be sending you my list of Jamison folks that I need to talk with." Then he added "but only after I see your documents." His tone was evident by the smirk that came with the comment.

"Have a nice day Matt," Davidson said as he turned to leave.

Matt waited. At least until he knew that Davidson was well on his way. He didn't want to have to run into him again today.

CHAPTER 2

Matthew James Taggart had been a lawyer at Olimeyer, Barkley & Smith for six years, a good year away from coming up for partner and still enough of a whipping boy that he was sent to handle court appearances that the partners didn't want to attend. Matthew, or more often just called "Matt," was 32, relatively lean, about six feet tall and was just starting to show some grey hair. He still had a full head of hair which he thought was a positive sign since it seemed that most of his contemporaries that practiced law had already lost theirs.

In college, Matt had worked pretty hard, but also had time for a fraternity life and played some intramural sports. He had been a pretty good baseball player. Since law school and over the last few years he had given himself less and less time for sports, although he occasionally played softball in the summer lawyer's league. Matt was a switch hitter and he was well regarded for his hitting more then his fielding.

Matt had been a decent middle-of-his-class student in law school, but his father's connections had opened up the door for him at the firm. Since Matt had started at the firm, he had worked his ass off as an associate, getting involved in some of the firm's biggest cases, but he was still a long way down the ladder in the firm's hierarchy.

O, B&S was a 50-lawyer boutique litigation firm. It handled large complex insurance defense matters most of the time, like the case Matt was working on now involving a claim that his client's new drug for menopause resulted in sudden heart seizures. Although Davidson's firm had only brought this one case for a 53 year-old woman who suddenly died after taking the drug for a week, Davidson contended in his filed complaint that Jamison has doctored its clinical tests to get FDA approval for the drug. If he was right, it would open the door to a class action lawsuit that would involve over 200 women who had taken the drug and were now claiming they had suffered heart damage.

When he arrived back at the office, his first stop, before he even took off his coat or put down his briefcase, was to go directly into the office of name partner Dwight Smith to tell him the bad news from his earlier visit with the Judge.

"Dwight, you have a minute?" Matt rapped softly on the partly opened office door.

"What happened? You should have been back an hour ago," Smith yelled.

"I stopped off at the Clerk's office to file some papers in another case." Matt had actually stopped at Starbucks on the way back to get a break since he knew what he was in for when he got back to the office.

"So, what happened?" Smith asked, not even looking up from the papers on his desk.

"It wasn't good. He wants a production or a good faith basis response in two weeks," Matt outlined.

"Did you tell him what I told you to say about proprietary information?" Smith demanded.

"Yes, but he wants something specific. He's going to order the production." Matt was looking at the top of Smith's head since he had still not looked up.

"Shit!" Smith said loud and clear, deliberate enough that Matt knew what was coming next. "I do not want to produce those documents. You need to find a way to block that production. I don't want to give in that easily."

"What do you want me to do?" Matt asked back, now looking at Dwight Smith eye to eye.

"Get the research done to stop the production . . . stall, all the way to the Supreme Court if you have to. Jamison does not want us to produce those documents. We need to keep Davidson from seeing those records." Smith now rose from his desk, his five foot-six, 220 pound overweight frame now hovering over his desk. He was sweating from his armpits and his face was red and blotchy.

"What should I tell the Judge?" Matt asked.

"Anything you want. But we can't produce those documents. We won't produce them." Smith was starting to pace back and forth behind his desk.

"Dwight, you're setting me up, aren't you?" Matt's question coming out more like an accusation.

"I tell you what to do and you do it, are we clear Matt?" Smith was now barking orders.

"You've got to learn to how to handle adversity, Matt. You gotta learn sometime." Smith then added. "I want to see a draft of something by the end of the week."

Matt just wanted to hit him, right there. Just cock back and clock him one, but he turned around, took a deep breath, picked up his briefcase and walked out of the office. "I'll get on it." Matt said under his breath. As Matt walked down the hall from Smith's office on the way to his two-window associate office, he passed his secretary and asked, "anyone looking for me?"

"Well, I guess you already saw Dwight. Sorry about that. Tom wanted you to stop by to see him sometime today. Nothing urgent, about the Amtrak case . . . and Linda called."

Tom was Tom Barkley, another one of the name partners, a little more easy going, but still pretty demanding. Linda was Matt's wife.

"Got it. Thanks." Matt sat down at his desk. As he was reviewing some of the faxes that were on his desk and some interoffice memos on his e-mail, he pressed the number one on his speed dial.

"Hello," came the voice from the other end.

"Hi, honey. What's up?" Matt asked.

"Nothing, really. You just didn't seem too happy when you left this morning."

"Well, I just knew that I was going to get screwed by the Judge. Thanks for calling. How's Sally feeling?"

"Better, I think. She's napping now. Fever's down. I think she'll be better tomorrow. What time will you be home?"

"I won't. It looks like I'll be working on this Jamison case for a while. Sorry."

"Not like it hasn't happened before. Call me tonight, okay?"

"Sure. Bye," Matt said.

Matt had already hit the intercom button for Tom Barkley before his wife had a chance to say goodbye.

CHAPTER 3

Linda and Matt had been married for three years. They had met first when he was finishing law school at Georgetown University, but didn't meet again until he was already in his second year at Olimeyer. They were married a year later.

Matt would always tease Linda that she hung out at the bars in Georgetown waiting to meet a future doctor. Unfortunately for her, she met a lawyer. They dated a few times before he started work at Olimeyer and then broke it off when Matt was spending more time at the office then with her. He saw her again at a party about a year later and both of them realized they were better off together then they were apart. They got married at her family's house in Richmond. It was a wonderful event. All of their friends were there and Matt's parents got along great with Linda's.

They decided to buy a small house in Bethesda so that Matt could take the Metro into the office instead of driving every day. Matt worked pretty long hours and sometimes Matt and Linda didn't see that much of each other. After a year, Linda had gone back to school at the University of Maryland to get her masters in social work, but then she got pregnant with Sally. When Sally came along it had changed everything. Linda stayed at home and Matt worked even more then before. Bigger cases, more hours, more stress. Although Linda wanted him to be home, she seemed to understand. Maybe because she knew that part of Matt's happiness, or at least part of his presumed happiness, was tied to his success in his career. For whatever reason, Matt and Linda seemed to make it work.

CHAPTER 4

Senator Jason Taggart turned his Lear 678 Turbojet plane south onto Runway 6, and called the Tower.

"Charlie Delta 475 ready for takeoff on Runway 6 south."

"Roger, 475, you're next in line."

"Thank you, Tower." As he waited, Senator Taggart thought about all the problems he was leaving behind him in Washington, at least for the weekend.

"475, okay for Runway 6 south. Have a good flight, Senator," the Tower called in.

The Senator pressed the pedals and pushed the throttle down, adjusting the flaps and checked the speed. At 124 mph he pulled back and the jet took off at a perfect 35 degree angle. The Senate had just adjourned for a mid-session break and Senator Taggart was heading back to Charlotte for a week at home. He had only a few local meetings scheduled and hopefully some time for golf. He needed a break.

Jason Taggart had been flying since 1953. He joined the navy after High School to learn a mechanical trade and was moved into the aviator program when he passed some required math tests. He became a cargo pilot in the last months of the Korean War and then flew two tours in Vietnam. After his election as a congressman from the 6th District that included Charlotte, he'd bought a small single engine Cessna and had been flying through his two terms as a congressman, and now as a senator. He had graduated up to this turbojet about three years ago. Although his wife was frightened for him when he flew by himself, she knew he would never stop. It was part of who he was. The flight would take two hours. Taggart thought he would take his flight line along the coast. Since he was flying at dusk, he caught a beautiful sunset of a red and orange sky as he reached 12,000 feet.

CHAPTER 5

It was already after 10:00 p.m. the last time Matt had looked at his watch while sitting in the firm library. He was researching the protections available for proprietary secrets. He was steadily getting pissed with the fact that Smith had sent him to research something that Matt knew he couldn't find and he was becoming antsy at the thought that Judge Lantham was going to rule in Davidson's favor and award attorneys' fees. Matt knew that Smith was going to blame him for the loss in front of Jamison. It was a no win situation.

Matt was in the middle of reading another factually complex trade secret case when his cell phone rang. He looked at his caller ID and it said "home." Then he looked at his watch. It was now almost eleven o'clock.

"Hello?" he answered.

"Matt, something has happened to your Dad," Linda said.

"What? What happened?"

"It's on CNN. He was flying from D.C. to Charlotte. He was supposed to have arrived over three hours ago. The plane dropped off the radar screen. They're sending search planes."

"Oh my God. Not Dad. Was my Mom with him?"

"I don't know," Linda answered. "You need to see this. Please come home."

"Let me call the house first. I'll be home as soon as I can." Matt hung up the phone and then tried to dial his parents' house in Charlotte, but with all the adrenaline pumping, he couldn't punch in the numbers right. It took him three times to get it right. He listened as the phone kept ringing.

"Taggart residence. May I help you?"

"Margaret, is that you? It's Matthew. Is my Mom there?"

Margaret was his parents' housekeeper. She had been with his family since Matt was born. "Oh, Matthew, I'm so glad you called. Your Mother, she's so upset, so scared. Here, I'll have you talk to her."

"Thanks, Margaret. You take care of her, okay?"

"Yes. Yes, I will." She said. Matt knew she was true to her word. She had already stood by his mother for years, especially when his mom was recovering from some kidney surgery she had a few years ago.

He was so relieved to hear that his mother was there. Now, onto his Dad.

"Matt?"

"Mom, are you okay?" Matt asked.

"Oh, dear God, they can't find your father."

"I know, Mom, I heard. What happened?"

"He called me this afternoon. He was flying the plane to Charlotte. He was coming home for the week. I was abrupt with him. I was late for an appointment, and I was so curt to him on the phone. Oh, my God, Matt, what am I going to do without him?"

"Hold on, Mom. Everything will be all right. Is there anyone there from his office?"

"No, no, not yet. Roger is here with Marcia, and someone is flying in from Washington. Someone from the F.B.I. is here, too. They said its standard procedure with a senator. Oh, Matt, can you come here?"

"Sure, Mom, let me speak to Roger." Roger was his older brother, he was 44, and was the eldest of the three children. He lived in Charlotte with his wife and two kids.

"I love you, Mom," Matt said.

"I love you too," she replied.

"Hello?" A male voice answered.

"Roger, it's Matt. What's happening?"

"We don't know yet, Matt. Someone from the F.B.I. is here. We really just found out about this about an hour or so ago. They think the plane went down over the water. His flight path took him over the outer banks. That's where they apparently lost him on the radar. I think they're sending rescue planes and search boats. We're watching on CNN."

"Thanks, Roger. Take care of Mom. I'll get there as soon as I can."

The next call was equally as hard. Matt dialed his sister and brother-in-law's number in Boston. She was expecting and the baby was due in less than a month. He dreaded this call.

His brother-in-law answered the phone.

"Hello? Ted? It's Matt."

"Matt, we just spoke to Linda. We know."

"How's Jenny?"

"She's resting now. She was out of control when we heard."

"I just found out," Matt said, "I've been holed up in the office."

"What happened?" Ted asked.

"I don't know. They said it just fell off the radar. The F.B.I. is at my Mom's house."

"Do they suspect foul play?" Ted asked.

"Too early. Mom says it's standard procedure. I'm going to try to get there tonight or in the morning. When Jenny wakes up, will you tell her I called?"

"Yeah, sure Matt. Let me know what you find out, okay?"

"I'll call you." Matt promised.

About thirty miles away in an estate home overlooking the Potomac River a phone rang twice. On the third ring the man, who had been staring at the phone as it rang, reached to pick it up. He put the phone to his ear and before he spoke, he took another puff on his Cuban cigar and placed the half smoked cigar down on the ashtray next to the 100-year-old scotch he had been drinking.

"Yes," the man gently said.

"The Senator's plane . . . it has disappeared. They're searching for it in the Atlantic" The voice on the other end of the phone was unemotional and direct.

"Yes, I know." The man said. Then he continued, "and let's hope they find it."

The man then hung the phone down and reached again for his scotch. "This calls for a drink," he said to himself. He smiled and leaned back further in his chair.

CHAPTER 6

It didn't take Matt long to organize his research and to leave a message for the firm librarian to copy the cases he had marked and for her to leave them in his office. He wrote out a message to his secretary that he had to leave town for a family emergency and left it at her desk, choosing not to use the firm e-mail system which certainly would have been more efficient but not as personal. As he was filling up his briefcase to leave, he thought about the deadline on the Jamison court order. He sat down at his desk again but this time typed an interoffice e-mail directly to Smith. It read "Dwight, I have a family emergency. I do not know when I will be back in the office. I'll be able to do the Jamison research but will need more time. Can you ask the court for a continuance? I will call in. Thanks—Matt."

As he typed the words, he realized that he could lose his job over this. It always crossed his mind that he got this job only because his father was in politics. He always felt it, but tried not to believe it. His father had always told him "I might open some doors for you, but you'll have to walk through them." That was why Matt has always worked so hard, either to prove to himself that he earned his own way or to honor his father's efforts to help him. Either way, his father had motivated him.

Tonight, as he walked out of the large glass doors of his office building, thoughts were screaming through his head about the plane, his father and even flashes of what might be happening at the crash site. He decided as he was walking to his car that he had to go first to help find his father and then he would go home to be with his mother. His brother was already there, and he needed to be where his father was. He would go to him first.

As he exited the parking garage of the office tower, he dialed his cell phone for Linda. She picked up on the first ring. "Matt, they have reporters there and helicopters flying over the water. It's on all the stations now."

"Where is the search?"

"Somewhere outside of Nags Head, North Carolina. Right off the coast."

"I'm going there first," he said.

"To Nags Head? Why?" Linda asked.

"I need to help find him."

"Honey, please come home," she begged him.

"I'm on my way," Matt answered.

"I love you," she said. She was crying on the phone.

"Me, too," he said. "It will be okay."

It was already after midnight and from his car Matt called the reservations number for Delta Airlines, expecting there to be some flight the next morning directly to the outer banks. He realized after a long conversation with the reservations agent that the best he could do was a 7:30 a.m. flight to Raleigh, North Carolina and a long rental car drive out toward Nags Head. He booked the flight. As he drove home he listened to the news on the radio. The disc jockeys were discussing the crash, along with issues like how this would affect the balance of power in the Senate and who would be the likely candidates for his father's seat. They also talked about Senator Taggart's role in Washington and his more notorious positions on issues like abortion, budgetary spending and tax cuts. They'd obviously been pulling this information off the Senate web site. The story became not whether he was alive or dead from the crash but whether the country would be better off without him. Matt turned off the radio.

CHAPTER 7

By eight o'clock the next morning Matt was on his way to Raleigh on Delta flight 332. The plane was a 727 and partially empty, likely because most D.C. travelers would take the later flight so they wouldn't have to get up so early. It didn't really matter to Matt since he didn't sleep anyway, not because he wasn't tired, which he was. It was mostly out of the guilt of having the luxury of sleep while the search parties were out there trying to find his father. His night was filled with talking to Linda, talking to his brother, brother-in-law and some close friends. The baby had slept through the night and all Matt got to do was reach in the crib to kiss her and tell her that he loved her. Then he said, "I hope you get to see your grandfather again." His stomach turned when he said that, since he started thinking about his dad more clearly and what it would mean if he was really gone.

Linda finally had gone to bed about 3:00 a.m. and Matt stayed awake watching CNN for news about the search. Matt left for Reagan National at about five o'clock. He couldn't read or think too clearly during the flight. The front page of The Washington Post already had some stories about the crash, some features about the Senator's life and some smaller articles about aircraft safety, the chances of sabotage, his father's flight safety record, and the normal crap when someone goes down in an airplane. The flight was only an hour long and although it seemed to last forever, the plane was heading down for landing with tray tables up before he knew it. He realized that he had lost track of time and actually dozed off during the flight, with his lack of sleep the night before and from the little sleep that he had gotten the last few weeks while handling the Jamison case.

Matt pulled some papers from the outside pocket of his briefcase to look at his notes he had taken about getting a rental car. He had called the one eight hundred number for Budget at about two o'clock in the morning and had reserved a car for pickup at the airport. He also looked at the maps that were displayed as illustrations in the newspaper to confirm that he was going to the right place. He planned on also getting a map from the rental counter. The process of getting the car and starting out on the drive didn't take too long and Matt was on the road to Nags Head in less than thirty minutes after the plane landed. When the rental car agent noticed his name, she asked if he was related to the man in the news. When Matt told her it was his father, she upgraded him to a larger car, and even though he didn't need the larger car for his ride, he thanked her just the same.

He made it to Interstate 16 and then onto State Highway 4 without to much trouble, noting the multitude of Waffle Houses and Stuckeys along the way. He called Linda the first time after he had landed to let her know that he was on his way. He called her the second time not really to say anything, but more to hear her voice and to check on Sally. Life just seemed a little bit more precious right now.

CHAPTER 8

While he was driving, all that Matt could really think about was his life growing up in Charlotte with his mom and dad and his brother and sister. He could see snapshots in his mind of his parents at his baseball games, being with him to visit his older brother at college and trips to Washington for inaugurations. His mind was a collage of images and he felt troubled by the fact that he couldn't remember more. He pictured his wedding with Linda and the fun his Dad had making the toast at the rehearsal dinner. He remembered Jenny's wedding and his Dad dancing with her.

Then intermixed with those images were the ones of what Matt expected to see at the crash site. He had seen the helicopter footage on CNN and the lights that glowed in the night sky as boats worked their way around the suspected crash site. He felt sick and he felt sad.

As Matt approached the area of the coast where the plane was thought to have crashed, he was stopped about a quarter of a mile from the beach because the police had created a roadblock to limit access to the area. Since the story had hit the wires, reporters and rubberneckers alike were arriving at the crash scene, some with responsibilities, others only with pure morbid curiosity. Reporters had also made their way to the Senator's house in Charlotte to interview Matt's mother and even more were stationed outside of Congress to get reactions from his colleagues and other Washington insiders.

Matt pulled up to the roadblock in his car and was stopped by a policeman at the checkpoint. Matt lowered his window and the policeman approached the car. "I'm sorry, sir, you can't go past here. You'll need to turn around."

"I'm Matthew Taggart, Senator Taggart's son. I need to get in to see the F.B.I. agent in charge."

"Can I see some ID?" the officer was impatient, he obviously had already been bombarded with requests to get closer to the site.

Matt pulled his driver's license from his wallet and handed it over to the policeman.

"Okay. I need to call this in. Please wait here sir."

Matt waited for about three minutes, but what seemed like an eternity as he watched the policeman on his radio speak to someone that was clearly giving the orders. The policeman then walked back towards Matt's car.

"Sir, I'm going to get you an escort to our base of operations at the Sheriff's office."

Matt thanked him and waited for the cruiser to pass around in front of his car. The first policeman leaned in toward Matt's window and said, "Please follow that car to the Sheriff's office."

Matt followed the police vehicle in front of him for about eight or nine blocks until the car turned into a gravel driveway which led up to the Sheriff's office. Matt could see a sign reading "Wilmington County Sheriff" which included movie marquee lettering announcing Terrence R. Clayton, Sheriff. The police car stopped around back and Matt pulled in alongside him. The police officer got out and invited Matt into the building from the back entrance.

While Matt was walking with the officer he asked him if he had heard anything about his father. "Not yet, sir" the tall gangly man responded. It was then that Matt could see the youth in the officer who was escorting him into the building. He figured maybe 19 or 20. "Thanks for your help," Matt said as the officer led him through the building to the second floor and to a door marked with the same marquee lettering. This time it was etched in the glass announcing "Terrence R. Clayton, Sheriff."

The officer knocked twice on the opened door. "Sheriff, Mr. Taggart is here." The young officer addressed the older man sitting behind a desk in a large wood laminate paneled office. There were framed pictures and plaques covering the walls.

"Okay, Kelly. They need you back at the roadblock. Report there until your shift ends at 7:00 p.m." The gray-haired man had a clear southern tone in his voice. Matt was thinking "Buford Pusser."

"Yes Sir, Sheriff" the young man responded.

As the officer turned to leave, Matt said, "Thanks again for your help, Officer."

"Good luck, sir," he said.

"Thanks. I think I'll need it," Matt answered.

Sheriff Clayton waived the formalities right from the beginning. "Let me tell you where we are, son. A radar tower picked up your father's plane about 50 miles north of Nag's Head. He was taking the coast route south, and his flight plan showed he would move west after he passed the outside island marker. Instead, the plane looks like it just dropped off the radar screen. We aren't sure if the plane kept to the flight plan, because we lost radar under 1,000 feet. We've established a search quadrant of fifty square miles, and the Coast Guard has been dispatched."

The Sheriff continued his report. Matt just was listening. "The plane was assumed lost at 8:00 p.m. last night and we believe there was a splashdown in this general area," the Sheriff now using his index finger to point to a location on a map laying across his desk. "It may still be a few hours before we can find any debris if it went down over the water. It's a big area and a small plane."

"I'm sorry," the Sheriff went on, "but even if it was a controlled landing, he has no raft apparatus on board, the water is pretty cold out there this time of year, and factoring in his age . . . well, we aren't very optimistic if the reports are accurate."

"I understand, Sheriff. I appreciate your honesty," Matt said. "I guess we're all expecting the worst but hoping for the best. You don't know my dad, but he can be a real hardass sometimes. He might surprise everyone."

"Let's hope so, but again, we may not know anything for a while." The Sheriff was trying to be nice. It was obvious to Matt. He just wasn't sure if the man was acting this way since they were talking about a U.S. Senator or because they were talking about a likely death.

"Thanks," Matt said, "but if it's not too much trouble, I'd appreciate if I could go ride along on one of the boats for the search."

"I'd like to help you out, but it's against policy to take civilians out there, especially during an operation like this," the Sheriff answered.

"I understand, Sheriff."

Then Matt rethought the situation. "Excuse me Sheriff, I need to make a call."

"Just let me know if there's anything you need, son." The Sheriff tried again to be nice. "I suggest you head back into town and find a hotel room. It may be awhile before we know anything."

Matt shook the Sheriff's large weathered hand and walked out of the office, down the stairs and back outside the building. There was a wet, damp chill in the air. Matt took out his cell phone and called to his mother's house in Charlotte. It was now close to noon. The phone was picked up on the second ring.

26

"Hello? May I help you?"

"Who's this?" Matt asked. He didn't recognize the male voice.

"I'm sorry, who's calling, please?"

"Matthew Taggart, the Senator's son. Who is this?"

"Agent Frank Jackson, F.B.I."

"I'm glad you're there. Who's the agent in charge?"

"Agent Dixon. D.C office."

"May I have his phone number please? I need his help."

"Certainly, Sir," the agent replied.

Matt wrote down the number.

"Thank you," Matt said. Then he asked "What's the situation there?"

"We have it under control. The area around the house is restricted. We've had some media problems, but they're behind the lines."

"Thanks again for your help." Matt hung up the phone and called Dixon.

CHAPTER 9

About an hour and a half later, a black sedan pulled up the gravel driveway and parked in front of the back door of the Sheriff's office. The man who emerged from the car moved quickly into the building. Matt was not surprised to see the man dressed in the dark suit and black raincoat, although he was a bit surprised that he had arrived so quickly. Sheriff Clayton was clearly pissed off that Matt had gone over his head about joining the search team.

"Mr. Taggart, I'm agent Jonas, FBI."

Matt shook the man's hand.

"Agent, this is Sheriff Clayton," Matt gestured to the Sheriff.

"Good to meet you, Sheriff. We have clearance to have Mr. Taggart join the search."

"I still don't think this is a good idea" the Sheriff protested. He was marking his territory. It was an obvious vain attempt for the Sheriff to keep his authority intact. The agent understood.

"This is an unusual circumstance Sheriff. I appreciate your cooperation. The Director wants to thank you for doing such a fine job here."

As soon as Sheriff Clayton heard the word "Director" he stood more erect.

"Well," the Sheriff continued, "I just don't want to see anyone get hurt out there."

"Yes, I understand." Jonas said. "We'll take it from here."

"Thank you again, Sheriff," Matt said, extending his hand.

"You're welcome, son." The Sheriff took his hand and shook it.

Both Jonas and Matt then walked out the back door and into the FBI agent's car. As Jonas backed the car away from the building, he said, "Your Mother apparently has friends in some high places."

Matt responded, "I think she plays Mah Jong with the Director's wife." Matt was trying to make light of his family's connections. "She really wants me to find out what happened to my father."

Jonas responded, "I understand, sir."

"What office are you out of?" Matt asked.

"I'm usually in the D.C. office. I was actually already in Raleigh on another matter. My team was called in on this matter and we were heading here anyway."

"Is the FBI handling the investigation?" Matt asked, curious at determining whether the FBI or Sheriff Clayton was running the show.

"No, we're simply here as observers, not an official F.B.I. presence. If we did, the media would light this up as some sort of criminal activity. We're here to observe and cooperate." Then he added, "It will change obviously if we determine there was foul play. Until then, we just watch."

"Where are we heading?" Matt asked.

"The search and rescue boats are leaving off the Highland Pier. We're only a few miles away."

Matt said "Thank you," and then he asked "Do you know anything more?"

"Sorry, sir, they're still narrowing the search area, but they believe they've found parts of the plane about a half mile from Nag's Head."

"It doesn't look good, does it?" Matt's tone was quiet.

"You never know." The agent responded.

"Thanks. I understand. Can I get out to the search area?" Matt asked.

"Yes, sir. The Coast Guard has a boat waiting for you that's going to be heading out to the target area. The Coast Guard and the N.T.S.B. are heading up the search." Jonas said.

"NTSB?" Matt asked.

"National Transportation and Safety Board," was the agent's response.

"Of course, right," Matt shook his head.

"Have you ever been involved in something like this before?" Matt asked.

"Plenty of accident scenes. We've had V.I.P. losses before, but not aircraft related."

Matt and the agent continued some small talk until the vehicle pulled up at the dock area. Numerous cars, boats, ambulances, EMS services and police were on the scene.

"There's a Coast Guard boat that's waiting. Let me park here and I'll get you on board," Jonas said.

After the agent parked the car, the two men got out and Jonas escorted Matt up the dock area to the waiting cruiser, which was about 65 feet long with a crew of six, soon to have a crew of seven.

Agent Jonas introduced Matt to Commander Sawyer who was heading the Coast Guard search and rescue mission from their base in Nags Head. Sawyer explained to Matt that the Coast Guard was coordinating its efforts with the N.T.S.B who had federal jurisdiction for these types of accidents. The Coast Guard officer explained that they were heading out to a target area where some other cruisers had spotted some limited wreckage.

The ride out to the search area was like a roller coaster ride without being strapped in. Matt could see the white caps and the four foot swells indicating the rough water. If the water had been any rougher the search would have been called off. Matt definitely didn't have his sea legs and he spent most of the 30 minutes it took to get to the area lying down on one of the cots below deck. As he lay there, Matt remembered a fishing trip that he had taken with his father and brother only a few years earlier in the Bahamas, before he was married. The seas were a lot calmer then, but he had planned in advance and taken some motion sickness pills. He had still gotten sick on the boat. This time, he hadn't gotten the chance to take anything before climbing aboard and he would never have asked since he didn't want to give anyone an excuse not to let him come along. One of the junior officers saw him lying down below deck and commented "you're better off topside, at least you'll get some fresh air." Matt took his advice and walked up the stairs to the main deck just as other boats in the area came into view. Matt realized as he came closer to the so called "target" area and saw some floating debris from the plane that the operation would soon change from a search and rescue mission to one of simply retrieval. Matt already felt as if his stomach was in his throat. This only made him feel worse.

CHAPTER 10

The boat approached the scene which already included another Coast Guard vessel from the Nags Head base. Matt was told by Commander Sawyer that sonar from the search vessel had located an image about eighty feet below the surface resting on a tiered area of the ocean floor. The image matched the general outline and size of the aircraft they were searching for. A team consisting of a Coast Guard diver and N.T.S.B diver had already been deployed to the plane.

Sawyer explained to Matt that the Coast Guard diver had the responsibility of locating any passengers in the aircraft. The N.T.S.B. diver was responsible for locating and retrieving the flight recorder that was stored in the plane. Once recovered, the N.T.S.B. diver would be responsible for the custody of the recorder for evidence purposes.

Matt then heard radio contact from the divers to the larger Coast Guard vessel over the load speakers of the boat.

"We have contact, Base One."

"What do you have, Remote One?"

"We've located the plane."

"Condition?"

"We have main fuselage. Looks like tail has separated. Still searching for the second section."

"Location of pilot?"

"Positive, Base One. Still strapped in."

"Any other passengers?"

"Negative, none located."

"Box located?"

"Affirmative."

"Can you retrieve the box?"

"Affirmative. Fuselage in salvage condition. Box retrievable."

"Capture box and verify markers for retrieval. Can you locate other section?"

"We are looking, Base One."

"Affirmative."

As Matt listened to the Coast Guard conversation he understood the finality of the search that had lasted less then 24 hours. His father was dead. The search was over. Matt looked over the edge of the boat and watched the waves lap across the bow of the boat. He looked into the water, somehow believing that if he looked hard enough, he could see down the eighty feet all the way to his father's plane. It had originally been the uncertainty of not knowing if his father was alive or dead that troubled him and there was clearly a sense of relief that Matt felt in finally having an answer to that question. Now, all he wondered, was how it had happened.

Commander Sawyer approached Matt after it was clear that his father's body had been located.

"Mr. Taggart," Sawyer said, "I guess you understand what you heard."

"Yes Sir, I do," Matt replied, still looking overboard.

"I'm sorry you had to learn it this way."

"No," Matt said, "I wanted to be here. Thank you for your help."

"You're looking a little white," Sawyer said. "I'm gonna have one of the boys get you some coffee. You should sit down, we'll be heading back in a few minutes."

"Thank you."

Sawyer began to turn away and then Matt asked "when will they bring up his body?"

"It's treacherous waters out there today." Sawyer responded. "We might have to wait to get back down to the plane. We'll bring him up first and then send down the cranes for the plane."

"You're bringing up the plane?" Matt asked.

"It's part of the investigation," Sawyer answered.

Just then one of the junior officers approached Sawyer and interrupted him asking for his approval on direction and speed.

"Twenty knots, west," Sawyer responded and then he added "and get Mr. Taggart here some coffee."

CHAPTER 11

Matt returned to shore about an hour later and Agent Jonas was waiting for him at the dock.

"Mr. Taggart," the F.B.I. agent called out, "over here."

"Thanks for meeting me," Matt said. "They found the plane," He added.

"I heard," Jonas said. "I'm sorry about your father."

"Thanks. Thanks for helping me too. I'm glad I was there when they found him."

"Is it on the news yet?" Matt asked. "Do you know if I have time to talk to my family before it gets on the news?"

Jonas replied, "I hate to say it, but you'd better hurry. They might already be broadcasting."

Matt pulled out his cell phone to call his mother, but it didn't have a signal. He moved to the parking lot and the signal got a bit stronger. He dialed the number to his parent's home in Charlotte. He felt that his hands were sweating and he could feel a tightness in his chest as the number rang through.

"Hello?" It was Roger's voice. The signal was weak and Matt heard himself yelling through the phone.

"Roger, it's Matt. I'm at the scene."

"What have you found out?" Roger asked.

"I need to talk to Mom, Roger. It's bad news."

"Say that again Matt. You're breaking up." Matt thought Roger was yelling now.

Then as Matt walked further away he hit a full signal. Matt spoke in a quieter tone, "I said it's bad news"

"Damn. What did they find Matt?" his brother asked.

"Let me talk to Mom first." Matt asked politely to his older brother.

"Okay, hold on." Roger said.

"Matt?" his mother said, her voice sounding weak, "what's happening? Have they found your father?"

"They found the plane, Mom." Matt hesitated. He didn't know if he could say the words. "He was still in the plane Mom. He's gone."

There was silence.

"Mom? Mom?" Matt tried to reach her, to bring her back. But all he heard were muffled tears and soft crying on the other end of the phone. He waited a minute and heard Marcia's voice.

"Oh, Matt. Matt, are you sure?"

"Yeah, they'll be retrieving the body later. He was still in the plane. I didn't want Mom to see it on the news. You take care of her, okay? I'm going to stay here a little while longer and see if I can find out what happened."

"I'm so sorry Matt" his sister-in-law said.

"Thanks, Marcia. I'll call you later."

After Agent Jonas drove him back to the Sheriff's office to pick up his car, Matthew drove to the Seagull Inn, a local motel about two miles from the coast. The Sheriff had helped him find a place to stay while Matt was waiting for the F.B.I. and the room had been made up in time for Matt's arrival. The Seagull Inn was a typical beach type motel without the luxury of being on the water. It was circa 1950's and probably hadn't been renovated much since then. The lady that helped him check in lived at the Inn but she didn't own it. She was in her late

60's but over applied her makeup to appear as young as she could. She had a southern tone to her voice and was pleasant in her manner while she described the Inn and its limited amenities. Matt knew without even speaking about it that the Sheriff had filled her in on who he was and what had happened. Once he made it to the room, he decided that he would take a quick shower and wait for the call from Jonas notifying him that they had retrieved the body.

The shower was warm and Matt let the water pour over him for longer then normal while he tried to wash the events of the last day from his body. He closed his eyes and leaned his head and body under the shower head. He turned the faucet hotter while the images of his father's last minutes before crashing came seeping into his vision. Was he calm? Did he scream? Did he fight with the controls? What had happened up there and was it as horrifying as Matt was imagining it?

It seemed to Matt that he had been in the shower for hours when he turned off the water. He grabbed some towels, throwing one around his waist and another around his neck to dry off. He walked back into the room and picked up the remote control. He turned on the television. He surfed the channels, passing by old sitcom reruns and some infomercials and came to CNN headline news. Although the story at the time was about the recent adventures of some teen idol, the ticker that ran below it read "Senator from North Carolina dies in plane crash." He then turned to another station which also ran the local story of the search for the Senator's plane. Apparently they knew what he knew. The body had been discovered and it was being retrieved along with the plane's black box, so they could try to determine what had happened.

He reached for his cell phone.

"Hello." The woman's voice answered.

"Hi Hon." Matt spoke monotone.

"Matt, I heard. I'm so sorry. Why didn't you call me?" his wife asked.

"I'm sorry. So much has been happening. The Coast Guard let me on their search boat. I was there when they found the plane. They are trying to bring him up. I called my mother to let her know."

"Where are you now?" She asked.

"At a place called the Seagull Inn, a few miles from the coast. I need to stay here until they bring him up. I have no idea what happens then. I'm not even sure about the funeral." He spoke somehow expecting her to know the answers.

"His office will know. Don't worry about that. Just go see your mother." Linda knew what he needed to hear.

"How's Sally?" Matt asked.

"She's much better. No fever now." Linda replied.

"Great. Give her a kiss for me, will you?"

"Yes. Call me when you get to Charlotte. Okay?" Linda's voice trailed. "I love you."

"I love you too Hon," Matt replied. "I'll talk to you later. Bye"

"Bye" Linda said and Matt heard the line go to static.

Matt fell back on the bed after he hung up the phone, and it suddenly hit him that he was living this nightmare for real. How did this all happen? He kept wondering. He started to picture his father from the last time he saw him. It suddenly struck him that it was the last time they talked. Did they say goodbye? Did Matt smile as he walked away? Did his father know that he loved him? Matt realized things would never be the same. He also wondered how much everything would change.

Mat had been awake the last two days without sleep. It was only 7:15 p.m. but Matt was exhausted. He had intended to only take a short nap so he hit the clicker to turn off the television, propped a pillow under his head and closed his eyes. The next time he looked at the clock it was 5:00 a.m.

CHAPTER 12

Matt sat up in bed and watched some television, then decided he would go for a run. Running for Matt was his only real exercise in between work and home. Matt would try to get in a few miles every other day and, during the winter, he had a treadmill in the basement.

The air was pretty thick as he hit the road. The sun was just coming up and the sky had a red-orange glow that, along with the clouds, made the view a peaceful one. Matt quickened his pace as he thought about what would happen today, if they would be able to retrieve his Dad's body, if they would be able to discover why the plane crashed. Matt also thought about work, what he was missing and whether any balls would be dropped while he was away. Matt was frightened by the prospect of making mistakes, always had been. He didn't seem to be able to avoid the scrutiny of others. Everyone had expectations for him. His parents, Linda and now even Sally. He had to take care of her, support her. He couldn't let her down.

He ran about four miles and then, back in the parking lot of the Inn, did some stretching. When he made it back to the room, he jumped in the shower.

Matt got dressed and saw that it was only seven o'clock. He decided to go ahead and head back out to the crash scene to see if anything had happened. When he got to the roadblock he had to explain again who he was. He waited another five minutes before they let him through and he drove his car directly to the same dock from which he had taken the Coast Guard boat. He looked for anyone that might know anything. The dock was relatively quiet and Matt assumed the boats were still at the site. He walked along the dock just thinking about his father and wondered what it would be like when they brought him to shore.

Matt waited until 8:00 a.m. to call the pager number that had been given to him by agent Jonas. His cell phone rang back with two minutes.

"Hello" Matt said.

"Mr. Taggart. How can I help you?" Jonas responded.

"I'm sorry to call so early. Has anything happened?"

"I spoke with the Sheriff's office about 6:00 a.m. this morning. A dive team was heading out there this morning for the retrieval. We should know something in a few hours."

"Will you call me when you hear from them?" Matt asked.

"Yes sir, I will," the agent answered.

A half mile east of where Matt was standing a black plastic body bag floated to the top of the water accompanied by two coast guard sailors. The dive had been successful. First the body, next would be the pieces of the plane.

CHAPTER 13

His cell phone rang while Matt was eating a late breakfast at "Phil's," the local eatery about two blocks from the docks. Matt had finally gotten back his appetite after his boat ride.

"Mr. Taggart," agent Jonas said, "the body has been retrieved and is being held at the local morgue for identification."

"Where is the morgue?" Matthew asked. "I'll come there right now."

"Sir, why don't you meet me back at the Sheriff's office and we'll escort you from there?"

"How soon can you meet me there?" Matt asked.

"Twenty minutes," Jonas responded.

"I'll be there," Matt said.

When Matt arrived at the Sheriff's office, he was greeted by Sheriff Clayton. "Mr. Taggart, our condolences," the man said as he reached out his hand to Matt.

"Thank you, Sheriff." Matt responded. "Thank you for all your help."

"No problem, son. Give me a minute, and I'd like to join you over at the morgue. I need to bring some paperwork. Also we have some personal belongings for you that were brought up as well."

Matt waited while the Sheriff collected the necessary paperwork for identifying a body and then offered to drive Matt and the FBI

43

agent to the morgue, which was only a mile or so down the road in the basement of the County hospital. When they arrived at the morgue, Matt was brought into a small office where he was introduced to Dr. Stephen Bennett, the County's Medical Examiner. Dr. Bennett looked to be over seventy, with wisps of white hair and half glasses hanging over his long, thin nose.

Dr. Bennett approached Matt and explained to him that he would need to identify his father's body. Matt said he understood and then Matt, Dr. Bennett and Sheriff Clayton entered an adjacent room where a body was lying on a steel table covered in a large white sheet. Matt could see only an outline of a face where the sheet was draped across the body and Matt shuddered as he approached the table. Dr. Bennett walked up to Matt from behind and asked if he was ready before he moved back the sheet.

Matt responded, "I am."

As Dr. Bennett pulled the sheet back, Matt saw his father's face. His eyes were closed and he looked ashen and swollen, probably from being under the water for so long. Matt wanted to touch him, to say something to him, but he was unnerved by the other people in the room. Matt looked down to the floor. He then simply said, "it's him," and turned away. Matt then sat down in a folding metal chair in the corner of the room, sitting there in silence, thinking about his father. For a moment there, the thoughts came swimming into his head. He saw little league games. He saw his father in Congress and he remembered his first flight with him on his father's plane when he was twelve. He saw his father dancing with Linda at their wedding. He saw his father the first time he held Sally in his arms. His heart hurt. He couldn't believe his father was gone.

Matt knew, as Dr. Bennett wheeled the gurney away, that an autopsy would be taken by Dr. Bennett to determine whether his father had suffered a heart attack or stroke or some other physical condition that had led to the crash. Matt stood up and walked out of the room.

As he drove back to the Seagull Inn, the picture that went through his mind was one he had before, when he had heard about other plane crashes or had seen them on the news. What would I do? Matt thought, if I knew that I was going to crash and might die. "How would I react? What would I be thinking in the seconds before the plane hits the ground?" Matt shook his head trying to rid himself of the image. Matt just kept hoping that his father had not suffered.

When he got to the Inn, he called Linda. Matt started to describe his experience at the morgue. Linda was a good listener.

"I'm so sorry Matt," she said

"It's hard to believe, isn't it? How someone can be here one day, but gone the next?" Matt was choking up. "It didn't even look like him. I mean his body was bloated from the saltwater. He was all bruised up. I hated seeing him that way."

Then Matt said "I'm leaving for Charlotte in the morning."

"What should I do?" Linda asked.

"Let's wait to see where the funeral will be. It could be in D.C." Matt answered.

"Whatever you want honey. I want to be there for you. I guess it will be easier if I know, then I can figure out what help I'll need for Sally." Then Linda added, "I've been thinking. At least your Dad got to meet Sally."

"I was thinking the same thing," Matt said. "We have that picture, don't we, of Dad and Sally?"

"Yes," his wife answered, "we do."

Matt pictured the photo in his head. It meant a lot to him that he had it. One day it would be really special to Sally.

"Okay. Then I'll call you when I get to Charlotte." Matt said.

Linda said "I love you Matt."

"You too, honey."

Matt could hear that Linda was crying. He told her again that he would call her from Charlotte and then they said their goodbyes.

Matt then called his older sister. Jenny was 38 and was now pregnant with her first child. She had met Ted and gotten married almost two years ago when she was thirty six and it had taken her over a year before she had gotten pregnant. She was so happy about being pregnant. This was all so devastating to her.

Ted picked up the phone on the second ring. He saw Matt's caller ID on his phone.

"Matt? Hey, it's Ted."

"Ted. Hi. I just wanted to check in. How is everyone?"

"We're doing okay. How are you? Are you there?"

"Yes. I just came from the morgue. It was pretty bad."

"What happened?"

"They don't know yet. They're doing an autopsy and bringing up the plane."

"What about the funeral?"

"I don't know about that either. I'm leaving for Charlotte in the morning. I'll call you once I know the details."

"Okay. That's fine. I don't think we can travel anywhere anyway. I don't think Jenny is allowed to fly."

"I understand. Can I talk to her?"

"Sure. I'll get her. Good luck Matt."

"Thanks Ted."

Ted was also a lawyer, but a public interest type. He worked for a consumer products safety office in Boston. That's how Jenny had met him. She was not a republican like her father. Quite the opposite, she was a vocal democrat. She worked as a researcher and fundraiser for a private social action group and they had met during an event for a local democratic politician. Her interest in social issues had always made for interesting family dinner discussions, especially during her father's elections. Notwithstanding their occasional verbal sparing, which might have actually swayed her father on occasion, they each respected the others independent ideals. More then anything, Jenny loved her father. She always told him that.

"Matt?" Her voice was soft and a bit horse, probably from crying.

"Hey sis. How are you? How are you feeling?"

"I'm feeling a bit better. I just spoke to Mom and Roger a little while ago. I think it's great that you went there. I wish I could be with you. It must have been difficult to be there for that."

"Everyone's been really nice. You should get a load out of the local Sheriff though, it will make for quite a story."

"You know that I probably can't fly down for the funeral, right?"

"I know. Don't worry about it."

"But I feel terrible about that. Mom needs us."

"She needs a new grandbaby more. Especially now. Don't worry."

"Thanks Matt. How's Linda and Sally?"

"They're fine. Linda's waiting to travel until we know where the funeral is. It could be D.C.," Matt answered.

"But doesn't Mom and Dad have plots in Charlotte, at St. Mary's?"

"I don't know. It's kind of confusing, but I'll know more tomorrow when I get to Charlotte."

Then Matt added, "I love ya' sis."

"You too, Matt. Give my love to Mom."

"Will do. Take it easy for me, okay?"

"I promise. Bye," his sister said.

"Bye," Matt replied.

Matt put his phone down. He was tired of talking, but he had one last call to make.

He dialed the number and checked his watch at the same time.

It was now close to 5:00 p.m.

"Mr. Taggart's office, may I help you?"

"Janine? It's Matt."

"Matt. How are you?"

"I'm okay. I'm in Nags Head at the crash scene."

"We were all so sorry to hear what had happened."

"It will be a while before I can make it back to the office. Did Dwight get my message about the Jamison matter?"

"Yes. Dwight took the file back. He's already dictating the motion for continuance and I'm working on the pleadings. I understand the Judge was sympathetic about the situation when Dwight called the Judge's Clerk to notify him the motion for continuance was coming."

"Yeah, but Davidson will probably object. In any case, it won't buy us that much time. Not much I can do about it now."

"Matt, when's the funeral?"

"I really don't know. I am guessing that Senate services will be arranging it with my mother. I'm not sure if it will be in Charlotte or D.C."

"Please let us know. If it's here there are a lot of us that want to be there for you."

"I will. Thanks," Matt said.

Matt thought for a minute and added "I'll need for you to prepare those form motions for a leave of absence in my other pending cases. Ask for four weeks."

"You need me to do anything else?" Janine asked.

"Not that I can think of. Watch the mail. Let me know if anything is happening. I have my cell. Call me if you need anything."

"When are you coming back to D.C.?" Janine asked.

"I'm leaving for Charlotte tomorrow morning to be with my Mom. I guess it depends on when the funeral is. Hold the fort down for me, will you?"

"Take care, Matt."

"Thanks, Janine."

Matt hung up the phone and decided that he needed to get out of the room, get some air and get some dinner. He got into his car and headed for town. As he drove, he dialed a number on his cell phone and hung up. The return call came a minute later.

"Hello?" Matt said.

"Mr. Taggart, I got your message. How can I help you?" agent Jonas asked.

"First, please call me Matt."

"Sure. Okay Matt. What can I do for you?" The agent was still all business.

"I'm leaving for Charlotte in the morning," Matt said. "I was going to run out to have some dinner. Can I buy you a meal? I really want to thank you for all your help. Plus, I could use the company."

"Well, it's hard to refuse a meal that doesn't involve take out. Sure. Where're you heading?" Jonas asked.

"I'm not quite sure," Matt replied. "The motel clerk told me about a steak place that was pretty good on Harbor Street, it's apparently right off the town center. The restaurant is called the Grille."

"Okay, I'll find it," the agent said.

"Great," Matt said. "I'll see you there."

CHAPTER 14

Matt drove back to Raleigh and caught a 7:20 a.m. flight to Charlotte on a 18-person puddle jumper that took only 30 minutes from takeoff to landing to reach the Charlotte regional airport. His brother Roger was waiting for him at the gate when he arrived.

They greeted each other with a hug.

"Roger, it's good to see you," Matt said. "How's Mom?"

"She's trying to be strong. You know how she is. She has the whole community surrounding her. I've never seen so much food. She's taken control over the situation. She just keeps saying that she told him not to buy that plane."

"She did warn him, didn't she?" Matt said, recalling an infamous discussion during a large family thanksgiving dinner when he announced that he bought the plane.

"That was quite a fight. I remember it too." Roger said.

"I just can't believe that Dad did anything wrong with the plane. I'm worried that it was a heart attack or something," Matt said. "I know they're doing an autopsy."

"When will we know?" Roger asked.

"I don't know," Matt replied. "It shouldn't take that long I would think."

They walked to baggage claim and picked up Matt's bag and made their way to Roger's car waiting in Airport parking.

Matt tossed his one bag into Roger's SUV and hopped in the front seat.

Roger was backing out of the parking spot and Matt began asking about Roger's kids.

How's Tom? Matt asked. Tom was Roger's oldest son. "Great," Roger replied. "He's already a freshman in high school. Plays baseball and wrestles. He's pretty good, much better then I ever was." Roger was a proud father.

"How's he taking all of this?" Matt asked

"Not too well. He and Dad were pretty close. Every time that Dad was back in town they would get together. They would go to the Panthers or Bobcat games. Dad has . . . I mean had," Roger stumbled, "great seats."

Roger paid the parking fee to the attendant at the garage exit.

"And Sammy?" She was Roger's ten year old daughter. "How's she handling it?"

"She's taking it pretty rough. She's spending time with Mom. Mom likes having her around. I think it helps her to be with her grandchildren."

Roger took the airport road to the highway and lit up a cigarette.

"Marcia still on you to quit?" Matt asked.

"I gotta have a vice," his brother said. "But since we got the phone call I've probably smoked a carton already. This thing with Dad has really shook me."

"Me too," the younger brother answered, "but my answer is booze."

"Really?" Roger was amused. "You old enough to drink?"

"Hey big brother, don't mess with me. Remember, I'm a father now too." Matt said.

"Unbelievable. How'd we ever get so old?" was Roger's response.

"You know," Matt said, "whenever I come home, I do feel young again, like I'm eighteen back in high school. Do you ever feel that way?"

"Occasionally, but when you start dropping your son off at your old high school so he can go to the school dances, it brings you back to reality really fast."

Matt laughed. Then he asked "How's business?"

"Pretty good," Roger said. "The real estate market around here is starting to turn around. Investors are looking to dirt again rather then tech stocks to secure some of their money. I've been working on two commercial towers that are scheduled to be developed next year, just north of downtown."

Roger was a commercial developer. He had started small, but had gotten his break, just like Matt, when his father went into politics and money started to flow into the region for development and jobs. Roger got a lot of the contracts because of who he was related to. He had done well. Roger never ignored the fact that his father had opened the door for him too. Matt remembered again a dinner one night when they were all younger. His father spouting off his wisdom. He used to say things like "there's no such thing as a free lunch" or "I can just open the door, you have to walk through it." Matt remembered those. When he was younger he didn't understand the message. Now, he did and so did Roger.

"What has Mom said about the funeral?"

"I think she's said that it would be in Washington. She said his office would handle it."

"What do you think Dad would have wanted?" Matt asked.

"Nothing over the top, I can tell you that. But he does deserve the recognition." His brother replied.

Roger took the Maple Avenue exit off the highway and made his through the tree-lined road that led to Matt's old neighborhood. Matt looked out the car window and grew nostalgic as the car passed by houses where his close friends had grown up and he saw that those houses were owned by new, young families. Matt assumed that the only reason his parents had not yet sold their house was that his mother still entertained there for local political events.

As Roger turned up the driveway to his parent's house Matt felt his heart tug when he realized that his father wouldn't be there to see him when he arrived.

When Matt and Roger entered the house there were a dozen or so people that were gathered in the living room. An enormous buffet had been set up in the adjacent dining room. Matt saw his mother sitting on the living room couch and when she saw him, she rose and said "my Matty" and made her way to him to embrace him. He made but only two steps toward her before they met and hugged each other. She said "your father loved you so much Matt. He was so proud of you."

"I know Mom" was all Matt could do to respond. She then stepped back, looked at him and said. "Matt, you look so tired."

"I'm fine Mom. I really am," he said. "How are you?"

"I told him not to buy that plane. I did. I knew something like this would happen," she said.

"What did happen Matt?" she asked. "Do you know?" She looked at him as if he had all the answers.

"I don't know yet Mom. They don't really know. They're investigating it." Matt didn't want to mention the autopsy.

"Come have something to eat Matt. You must be hungry."

"Actually, I am," Matt said. "Thanks Mom." He kissed her on the cheek and then he walked toward the dining room. As he turned, he realized that his eyes had welled up and he began to wipe away the first tears that he had since learning about the crash. He had pushed it down somewhere in his gut while he was making the trip to the coast and when he identified his father. He had been businesslike, acting like a lawyer the whole time. But now the emotion was welling up, especially after seeing his mom. Matt wasn't sure if he would still be able to control it.

CHAPTER 15

Matt's time at home was bittersweet. It was always odd to be back in the house that he grew up in. Even though he was turning 33 he really did feel like he was back in high school again when he was home. Matt always said that he still felt twenty when he turned thirty. He hoped he would feel forty when he was eighty, but he wasn't so sure about that.

He walked around the old house and looked at the pictures of his family all along the walls up the staircase to the second floor, including his wedding picture with Linda. There were pictures of Roger at graduation, of Jenny in her wedding dress, of his mother with Roger's kids. He walked into his old room which was now being used by his mother as a storage room with all of the Christmas lights and wreaths that would be placed on the house in the winter. His high school diploma still hung on the wall and his high school trophies and other awards still sat on the shelves.

It was just a long walk down memory lane, made more painful by the realization that his Dad was gone from the life that he loved so much. It didn't feel the same to be in the house without the smell of his father's occasional cigar.

"Matthew?"

Matt heard the voice and recognized it immediately. He turned and saw her. "Margaret, how are you?"

Matt and the woman embraced and Matt knew right then that he was home. Margaret had taken care of him since he was a baby. He always said that she was his "second" mother.

"Oh, it's so sad about your father," she said. "He was such a good man. I'm going to miss him oh so much." Then she said "and your poor mother. That woman has been through enough already. But she's strong Matthew. She'll be all right." Margaret said.

"Only if you're there to take care of her Margaret," Matt replied.

They talked a bit more, about Linda and Sally and life in D.C.

"It's not like home." Matt said.

It was almost an hour later when Matt came back downstairs after talking more with Margaret and getting a chance to wash up. When he saw his Mom in the kitchen he asked her to sit down with him. Many of the well-wishers had left, but a few still lingered.

They sat at the kitchen table, his mother gazing out the window toward the backyard most of the time.

"How's Sally?" his mother asked.

"She's great Mom, Linda too. They'll meet us for the funeral. Linda sends her love."

"I love her," his mother said. "She's a great mother, isn't she?" His mother was just looking out the window.

"Mom, where will the funeral be?" Matt asked.

"His office is planning it. They said Washington. Your Dad wanted to be buried at Arlington Cemetery. We never bought plots here.

Matt knew that his father hardly ever spoke of death even when he once was recovering from a bout of pneumonia and he was in the hospital for a few weeks. He had talked about the fact that he had skirted death while flying in the war and that some of his buddies had not been as lucky. Matt knew that as a Senator and former Congressman, he would be entitled to be buried at the National cemetery even without his military service. But now, his father would be buried alongside other pilots he served with in Vietnam. Matt smiled at the thought that his father's wish would be fulfilled.

"Do you want more coffee?" His mother offered. She stood up and walked to the coffee maker sitting on the kitchen counter top.

"No thanks Mom." Matt said. "Do you known when?" he asked.

"I think they said it will be Sunday. You can ask David, his assistant. He's working on the plans. He'll tell you."

Matt could see how tired his mother was.

"The President might be there. They always got along so well," his mother added. "Matt, please have something to eat, you look hungry." His mother then walked out of the kitchen back toward the living room.

Later that afternoon Matt called his father's chief of staff David Wharton at his father's Senate office in Washington. David had been with his father since his first congressional race and had started as a legislative assistant out of college. He had gone to Harvard. Matt's Dad always said that David was smarter then he was. Then, over the last ten years, David had worked his way up to being his father's right hand man in the Senate.

He had to leave a message since David was out of the office, but the office offered to page him. David called back within fifteen minutes. It turned out that David was meeting with a staff member from the Congressional Special Services office who was handling the funeral arrangements for his father. David explained that his father's body would be flown from Wilmington directly to Washington. The funeral service would be held at the National Cathedral and burial would follow at Arlington. The funeral was scheduled for Sunday afternoon. It didn't leave them a lot of time, but the few days would allow just enough time to allow Senator Taggert's family to travel to D.C. and to allow the dignitaries who would attend sufficient time for them to clear their schedules.

Matt thanked David and each said that they would see the other at the funeral.

At about nine o'clock that night, Matt told his mother that he was borrowing her car and took a drive around the neighborhood. He stopped at his old high school and did a drive-by of the baseball fields. After about thirty minutes, he decided to drive into town to get a drink.

He parked in front of the Rose and Crown, a bar that used to be an old hang-out for him when he visited his parents during college. He walked in, looked around at the crowd and took a seat at the bar.

"What'll it be?" the bartender asked.

"Jack and Coke," Matt said.

Matt looked up behind the old English bar and saw that the game of the week was on, San Francisco versus Colorado. Barry Bonds was playing in the game and the Giants were winning by five in the fourth inning. Matt watched the game and enjoyed how smooth his drink went down. It had been a long day.

He ordered another and began to think through what the funeral would be like for his Dad. Matt kept imagining what he would do if he just had one more day to be with his Dad. There was so much that Matt still needed to ask him. Sally was just a baby and Matt wanted so much to talk to his Dad about what it took to be a father. Matt hurt at the thought of not having his father to talk to about his life and not having his father there to see his accomplishments. A lot of what Matt did he did for his father's recognition. Matt knew that. It didn't bother Matt. It had served him well. It had directed him through college and law school. It had grounded him when Matt had the risk of making stupid choices.

Matt just imagined whether his father was still watching him now. Matt lifted his drink and said "Dad, thanks for everything."

CHAPTER 16

By Friday the Coast Guard salvage team had located all the main components and structural parts of the plane. Unfortunately, the plane had settled in an unstable part of the seabed and with the depth of the plane and underwater wave activity the recovery of the structure and its parts was a dangerous one and had taken some extra time. The plane, including its engines, would be part of the accident investigation. The N.T.S.B. had already retrieved the black box, the recording device in the plane that captured all the information concerning the flight. Matt had remembered the transmissions he heard on the boat the same time they found his father. Although the plane was a relatively new one, the recorder only maintained flight information and did not include the cockpit voices as other larger planes did. The flight data recorder, as Matt had learned from Commander Sawyer, had an impact tolerance of 3400g's, a six year shelf life battery and a water pressure resistance of being submerged up to 20,000 feet.

Matt also understood, from his conversations with Commander Sawyer, that based upon the data from the traffic controllers that had tracked the flight, information that could be obtained from the flight recorder, such as the airspeed, altitude, heading and flap positions and the physical inspection of the plane, the NTSB, who was investigating the crash, would be able to determine the actions of the plane up to the time of the crash. That finding, combined with the physical inspection of the wreckage and the results of his father's autopsy, should allow them to determine the cause of the crash.

CHAPTER 17

Matt flew back to Washington on Friday afternoon. He missed Linda and Sally and felt that he needed to go home to ready things for the funeral. Roger and Marcia, Tom and Sammy and his mother would fly there on Saturday. Although his mother could have stayed at a hotel, taken care of by Senate Services, she decided that she wanted to stay at their townhouse on Capitol Hill. Her sister, from Atlanta, would be coming in for the funeral and would be staying with her in the townhouse. Roger, Marcia and their kids were going to be staying with Matt and Linda. Linda had fixed up the downstairs guest room for Roger and Marcia and their kids would crash in the basement, which Matt and Linda had finished and it was where they had put the big screen television. They would be fine down there on the pull out sofa and an air mattress. Regardless of the accommodations, it was nice that the family could be together.

Jenny had definitely been told by her doctor that she could not travel for the funeral. She was already experiencing some pre-term labor and the doctor would not let her take the chance. The doctor did her a favor, since without his stern warning, Jenny would have driven to D.C. just as easily as she could have flown. But she listened to her doctor. Her mother had weighed in too, telling Jenny to take care of herself. Matt had talked with her again to make her feel comfortable about not being there. He kept telling her that "Dad wouldn't have wanted you to risk hurting the baby." He also promised her that they would call her after the funeral to tell her everything. She agreed. Ted would stay with his wife. He told her that they could even watch the funeral on CSPAN.

On the day of the funeral, the cars had lined up so far outside the National Cathedral that additional security had to be brought in. It was a beautiful spring day. There were few clouds and a cool breeze. Flowers were everywhere and the tulips, now in full bloom, surrounded the cemetery. The Vice President attended the funeral in lieu of the President, who was touring Africa. Other dignitaries that attended included many of the congressional senators and representatives who had worked with Senator Taggart during his many years in the House and in the Senate. The chaplain from Matt's church in Charlotte officiated at the service and the Speaker of the House gave the eulogy. He spoke eloquently about the late Senator and his military service, his family and his work on behalf of the country. During the ceremony, Matt couldn't take his eyes off of his father's coffin, draped in the American flag.

The pole-bearers included Matt, Roger, David Wharton and congressman Eugene Decker, the former mayor of Charlotte who had taken Taggert's seat in the House when Matt's father ran for the Senate. The other men who had been honored with the task were former navy men who had once served with Matt's father in Vietnam. One was Charles Whitaker, who his father had once spoken about under the nickname "Woody" and Larry Foreman, his former co-pilot on some of his missions. Jason Taggart had once saved Foreman's life after their plane had been hit. Matt's father had flown the damaged plane back to the base and had managed to fashion a tourniquet around Foreman's leg at the same time. That deed had led to his father's silver star.

After the service, the procession of cars resulted in the closing of Pennsylvania Avenue and the Key Bridge. The limousine that carried Matt's mother and his aunt followed the black hearse. The next car was Matt and Linda, Roger and Marcia and their children. The next carried David Wharton and his wife Stacy. There were easily 100 cars, if not more, that followed the coffin to its final resting place.

As the family and friends gathered around the grave site, the minister read the final prayers. Roger stood to make a few final statements on behalf of the family, thanking everyone for their prayers, well-wishes and gestures of sympathy. He spoke about the forty-six years that his parents had been married, how his father loved his family and grandchildren and also loved his country.

Linda began crying when the bugler played taps and the flag was presented to Matt's mother. Elizabeth Taggert remained strong. She was the wife of a Senator and she held the course in his honor.

The Secretary of State, in his comments to the press after the funeral, called Jason Taggart the "ultimate humanitarian" for his significant role in approving appropriations for war-torn countries that needed financial aid. The Vice President applauded his fiscal wisdom and concern for others. One Senator said "he left us better off than when he found us." All of those comments would be repeated by the newscasters that covered the event and then later in The Washington Post. There was an estimate that a thousand or so people attended the funeral.

The reception after the funeral was held at the Capital City Club, a prestigious members only country club in McLean, Virginia. Senator Taggart, along with most of the U.S. Senators and Representatives were members of the club and its large clubhouse was a perfect location to offer guests the food and beverage called for after such a significant event. It was a party that Matt's Dad would have enjoyed, Matt told his mother. She agreed.

In one of the back rooms of the club, Matt sat with Linda, his brother Roger and sister-in-law Marcia and they looked through some of the photo albums that Roger had brought to Washington from Charlotte. Both Matt and Roger laughed at some of the pictures of their parents and their vacations. Roger recalled their trip to the Grand Canyon and the white water rafting adventure they took down the Colorado River. Roger poked fun at how Matt had fallen out of the raft and their dad had dished him out of the river.

"Yes, but don't forget the ski trip to Vail, big brother." Matt joked back.

Marcia and Linda began to "oooh and aaah." "This is getting good," Linda said.

"Okay, you win, I admit to being the only skier in the family that got lost on a blue run," Roger laughed.

"Lost, how do you get lost on a blue run?" Linda joked back.

"Hey, it was snowing, I couldn't see the markers. I got scared and turned around," was Roger's quick retort.

"Mom and Dad had the ski patrol out looking for him. He was missing for about three hours," Matt explained to the others.

"How did they find you?" Linda asked.

"Dad found me." Roger answered. Then he paused as if revisiting the moment in his mind. "He just retraced my steps and then, well I guess he was either lucky or smart. But when he found me he hugged me like I'd been gone forever."

"I didn't know that story," Linda said.

"Dad sometimes told it when he would talk about fatherhood to rotary groups and stuff like that. He won them over with the way he would tell the story." Matt said.

"How about Jenny? Any adventures with her?" Marcia asked.

"Matt, what about the time she climbed out the window to go out with that guy from college, the one Mom and Dad forbade her to see?" Roger said with a loud laugh.

"Right, we weren't there, but apparently my parents weren't too happy about a sixteen-year-old going out with a nineteen-year-old. Dad actually went to the local movie theater and had them stop the movie to find her. Jenny tells the story like it was the most embarrassing moment of her life," Matt added.

"The funny thing is that she did it again to them a year later," Roger said.

"Didn't Dad say he was going to put bars on her window once?" Matt laughed.

They called Jenny to talk to her about the funeral and tried to lighten their description of the day by filling her in on their walk down memory lane. She laughed a bit, especially about the movie story but then she cried. She reminded them that "Dad will never see my baby." They all knew that when the baby did come, the family would have to rally around Jenny to help her through it. It was a long day for all of them.

CHAPTER 18

After the funeral, Roger and Marcia and the kids stayed with Matt and Linda for another two days. One night all of them, including Matt's Mom and Aunt went out to dinner in Old Towne Alexandria at a local sea food restaurant. The next night Matt just cooked steaks and chicken on the grill. His Mother did not come over. She said she was too tired.

Wednesday afternoon Roger and Marcia packed up and Matt drove them all to his mother's house to say goodbye before he brought them to the airport. She was waiting in the townhouse courtyard for them when they arrived.

"Hey Mom, how are you?" Roger asked.

"Fine dear," his mother said. "I'm sad to see you go, even though I'll be back in Charlotte very soon."

"We'll make sure everything is taken care of at the house until you come back," Marcia said.

Tom and Sammy surrounded their grandmother and each gave her a hug and a kiss. Come home soon Grandma," they said.

After everyone had said their goodbyes, they loaded back up in Matt's car and Matt drove them to National Airport. Marcia and the kids went on. Roger stayed back to talk to Matt.

"Okay little brother," Roger said. "It's up to us now. We need to protect Mom and keep this family together."

"I know Roger. We will," Matt said. "I'll watch Mom here. I guess it will be your job back in Charlotte."

"No problem," Roger said.

The brothers hugged and Roger picked up his carry on and caught up with his family. Matt got back in his car and started the drive home. He pulled away from the curb just before he got ticketed for staying too long in the drop-off area.

Matt's mother stayed in Washington to make arrangements to pack up and try to sell the townhouse on Capitol Hill. Matt's mother and father had bought the townhouse on the "Hill" so they could stay together while the Senate was in session, although there were weeks where Elizabeth had traveled back to Charlotte to attend fundraisers and charity events and to see her friends. She had been in Charlotte for a week already when the accident happened. She had told Matt that they had been looking forward to the break in the session. She said that his father wanted to play golf and his parents had dinner plans with some close friends.

Matt had gone back into the office a few days after the funeral. He was welcomed back warmly by many of the lawyers and staff. There was a fruit basket on his desk along with some cards and some plants. Janine had left him a card sharing her sympathies with a note that said she understood his pain as a result of losing her father in a car accident just a year earlier. Later that morning even Dwight Smith had come to his office to shake Matt's hand and to share his condolences. Unfortunately, all that Matt could think of was whether Dwight was more upset about his father's death or losing the connection to the government work that he expected to get from hiring a Senator's son to work at his firm.

"What happened to the research on the Motion to Compel in Jamison?" Matt had asked Dwight.

70

"I handed it to Brian," who was another senior associate in the office, a guy that specialized in kissing Dwight's ass. "Lantham gave us an additional two weeks to respond because of your situation. He'll handle it." Dwight said, "I've got other work for you."

"Thanks Dwight." Matt answered. "I appreciate your help."

It took the rest of the morning for Matt to get through his unopened mail, unanswered e-mails and a list of phone messages.

At noon, Matt stopped what he was doing and left the office to meet his friend Eli at the Old Ebbitts Grill. Eli was a banker and they had known each other since Matt first started at the firm since Eli had started out working in the branch in the same building. Now, as Matt would say, Eli "hit the big time" when he got a promotion to handle wealth management clients for the bank.

It had been a few weeks since Matt and Eli had gotten together, although they had talked about the crash and Eli had attended the funeral. But now they had a chance to talk without the chaos.

Eli and Matt shook hands when they saw each other. Then Eli gave Matt a big bear hug. Eli laughed when he said "I love ya' man," taking a line from a beer commercial.

"No, you cannot have my beer," Matt said. "Or my wife." Matt added.

"Ooooh," Eli rebounded, "tough choice. I'll take the beer."

"Damn," Matt said. "I thought I had a taker." They both laughed.

They sat at the table and each ordered an iced tea.

"What, no shots?" Matt said.

"Hey, I don't start that until at least four o'clock. Remember, bank hours" his friend replied.

"I was always wondering why you guys closed so early," Matt said.

"So how are you doing Matt?" Eli asked, his friend taking a more serious tone.

"A bit distracted," Matt admitted. I've got a lot going on at work and I'm not really in the mood. I just got back and already Dwight's got stuff apparently lined up for me. I'm not sure they're going to put up with me if I don't start getting more done."

"They're not going to fire a Senator's son," Eli said.

"Ex-Senator," Matt reminded him. "Now they don't have that connection to power that they had before."

"So how's your Mom?" Eli asked.

"She's being much stronger than I thought she would be," Matt said. "She had so many people at the house after the accident and it really hasn't stopped since the funeral."

"Wow, that was really a funeral," Eli said. "I hope I get half that at mine."

Matt quipped "don't worry, your wife will bring a date." Matt always loved that joke.

"Speaking of wives," his friend retorted, when is Linda going to divorce you and run away with me?"

"Sorry old chap. You're not a doctor," Matt answered. "You couldn't afford her."

Both of them laughed.

After they ordered, Matt getting the cheeseburger and Eli the steak sandwich, the two friends continued their discussion of work, life and tried to schedule a time to make it to a Nationals game. Eli had tickets from the bank.

As they walked from the restaurant, Matt said to his friend "thanks Eli. I really needed this."

"Me too, buddy."

"I can't believe I have to go back today," Matt said. "I can only imagine what Dwight has waiting for me."

"Life's an adventure," his friend said as he shook Matt's hand and said "see ya."

Matt made it back to the office by 1:45. At four o'clock, Dwight came by Matt's office,

"You ready?" Dwight said.

"Guess so," Matt answered.

Matt followed Dwight upstairs through the back stairwell to one of Olimeyer's "war rooms." Dwight opened the door and Matt saw what looked like more than a hundred boxes of documents. Dwight explained that Jamison had delivered the boxes to Olimeyer's office in anticipation of Davidson's document production. Dwight explained that notwithstanding their effort to block the production that eventually Jamison would have to produce some, if not all of the documents that involved the history of Tribucal, its research and the testing that supported its FDA application.

Dwight went on to explain that if Lantham granted the motion to compel, that Davidson would want to review the documents right away. Dwight turned to Matt and said "review these and let me know if there is anything that could cause us trouble."

Then Dwight walked out.

"What a joy to be back" Matt said to himself as he looked across the room.

Although Matt was back, he had decided he wasn't going to overdo it like he had done in the past. He had talked to Linda about the hours, that he was going to cut back. He had told her that he had learned from his father's death that "life was too short."

He was still thinking the same thing when he looked at his watch and realized it was already seven o'clock. He had only managed to review ten of the boxes.

CHAPTER 19

Over the next week Matt came in late and tried to make it home early before Linda put Sally down to sleep for the night. He was sure that he was getting looks from the partners about his reduced hours, but they were apparently giving him some slack. He knew he'd see the damage at the end of the year when it came time to give out bonuses.

Since the funeral, Matt had visited his mother twice at her townhouse to help her with some of the packing and Linda had been by to visit with Sally. Since he and Linda had been married, Matt had been back to Charlotte only once, not including his last visit after the accident. He would usually see his parents every few weeks when they were in Washington. Now that his mother would be moving back to Charlotte for good, Matt knew that he would be seeing a lot less of her. He felt guilty about that. At least he knew Roger and Marcia and their kids would be there for her.

His time with his mother was sad. She spoke constantly about his father and the plans they had that would never happen. She worried about money, although they had plenty of it. She would always ask how she would manage without him. Matt spent most of the time reassuring her that she would.

It had been almost two weeks since the crash and questions clearly lingered with many as to how it had happened. The press continued with their stories every day. Was it human error, mechanical malfunction, or possibly even terrorism? The final answer seemed not to matter, especially since his father was gone, but the investigation couldn't be closed until a causation factor was determined.

CHAPTER 20

The National Transportation and Safety Board had completed its inspection of the wreckage. The process of retrieval and analysis had cost the taxpayers about half a million dollars. The goal of bringing up the entire plane was not only to assist in the investigation of the accident, but also to avoid the treasure hunters and looters who likely would have attempted to salvage part of the plane for money. The initial investigation of the wreckage, even though the plane was still partially intact, had been inconclusive. There were no signs of an explosion. The general condition of the plane did not indicate engine failure or other equipment failure. It had been verified from the radio control towers that tracked the plane from Washington that the Senator had made no radio call for help. Since the plane had a black box maintaining evidence of the instrument readings, it was hoped that the recording would provide the best explanation as to why the plane had crashed.

The N.T.S.B. had already held numerous press conferences about the accident, although those conferences were primarily limited to status reports about the progress of the retrieval of the plane. It was clearly government policy not to comment on causation findings until they were deemed conclusive. Over the years the N.T.S.B. had been accused of prematurely leaking information about certain accidents, especially in flight disasters where criminal activity was suspected. But now, the stories that were being circulated around the media and in Washington were something of an entirely different nature. <u>The Washington Post</u> had published an article citing an unnamed source that the accident investigation had progressed to the point that a definitive reason for the crash could in fact be determined but that the N.T.S.B. was delaying the publication of their findings. Rumors were rampant and ranged from sabotage from foreign terrorists to product failure, something about the rudder flaps.

Matt read in <u>The Washington Post</u> that the manufacturer of his father's plane had called for a special maintenance check of their planes that used similar Lockheed engines. He had also read that the F.A.A. was requiring additional security at all regional airfields which catered to private planes. But notwithstanding all the rumors, the N.T.S.B. simply maintained their public statement that the investigation was "continuing."

CHAPTER 21

It was after about 48 boxes that Matt finally thought that he was making some headway in the Jamison matter.

Most of the boxes dealt with the technology of the drug and the FDA application process. Matt was able to sort out most of the documents that went to the central issue of the case, the assorted results of the many clinical trials that Jamison held on the drug through patients who consented to take the drug or a possible placebo as part of their treatment. Many of the patients were over 50, but none were reported to have died from taking the medication. Matt started to outline all of the physicians who had been part of the study and all of the individuals who had kept records of the results.

Matt was actually enjoying this work. He thought of it as mindless. He didn't need to be doing it, but if there was a chance that Smith would lose the motion for protective order to block the production, they had to be ready to turn the documents over. So Matt continued to go through the documents cataloging what he found. So far Jamison looked to be in the clear.

CHAPTER 22

The phone rang at the home of the late Jason Taggart. Margaret picked it up and told the caller to hold while she found Ms. Taggart.

"Hello?" Elizabeth Taggart said as she took the phone.

"Mrs. Taggart. It's Leonard Nickels, from the NTSB."

"Hello Mr. Nickels. How can I help you?" she asked.

The call had lasted only a few minutes. She had told him he was wrong, that Jason would never do such a thing. She maintained her courtesy. She thanked him for calling. Then she hung up. She sat down on a nearby chair.

Nickels had called Mrs. Taggart in advance of a press conference. He had done it as a courtesy, since the news that the N.T.S.B. was about to announce was unusual. Nickels thought it would lessen the blow if he told Mrs. Taggart in advance of the conference. After she composed herself, she dialed Matt's number at his office. He wasn't answering so she asked for his secretary. Janine answered the call, spoke to Mrs. Taggart and told her that she would get him. Janine put the call on hold and ran, literally, up the stairs to find Matt.

She interrupted Matt while he was up to his neck in documents in the war room.

"Matt. It's your mother. She needs to speak to you now."

"What's wrong?" Matt asked. "Is she okay?"

"I'm not sure. It's about the NTSB and a press conference," Janine said.

Matt jogged back to his office and picked up the phone.

"Hello. Mom?" Matt asked. "Is everything all right?"

Her voice was shaking as she spoke. "Suicide," she said. "They are going to say it was a suicide."

"What? Who is going to say that?" Matt could hear his voice get louder as he spoke.

"The N.T.S.B." his mother said. "There's going to be a press conference."

The black box recording, Matt would learn from his mother, had confirmed the engine had been intentionally turned off in mid flight. The reports from the recording were considered to be conclusive. Senator Taggart had killed himself.

Matt's response had been the same as his mother's. He was shaken and incredulous. His father would never kill himself. The findings made no sense. He was sure that there must be some mistake.

Matt called Director Nickels to discuss his findings. When Nickels got on the phone he told Matt that they made a decision to issue the press release since they were feeling some pressure from the F.B.I. and F.A.A. that they could not hold back the announcement any longer. The government wanted the country to know that the crash had not been from terrorists or equipment failure and that it was safe to fly. Nickels apologized to Matt that they had no other choice but to make known their findings.

It did not take long for the news to spread that afternoon that the N.T.S.B. had concluded their investigation and had determined that the cause of the crash was "pilot error." When pushed on the specifics they had used the term "intentional downing." When asked if it was a suicide, they had responded that such a term was a "psychological one" and that they weren't psychiatrists. All they could say is that they found no external cause for the crash and found from the flight recorder that the systems had been manually turned off in mid-flight, leaving the plane in a glider like fall directly into the ocean where it was recovered.

Notwithstanding the words used during the press conference, the news was all over the airwaves concerning the "suicide."

Matt left his office and drove directly to his Mother's townhouse to calm her down. She had called him three times since the conference aired and she was getting call after call from the press to respond to the report. When Matt arrived at their townhouse, there were news vans parked outside and photographers stalking the front gate. Security now stood at the entrance to prevent photographers from gaining access to the courtyard that fronted the townhouse. Matt had to show the guards his driver's license in order to get into the house.

When he saw his mother, she was a wreck. It was the worst he had seen her since the crash. She had been crying and her mascara left her face almost black. She told Matt as soon as he walked in that "they are wrong! Wrong!" She kept saying over and over. "How could they say that about your father?"

"Mom," Matt began to speak the words that he had to say. "Is there something that I don't know about?"

CHAPTER 23

The office of the National Transportation and Safety Board was located on "M" street and 20th along with the other government agencies that consumed Washington, D.C. In the maze of bureaucracy that exemplified Washington, the N.T.S.B. was different in that it appeared to be caught somewhere between a law enforcement agency like the F.B.I. and a regulatory agency like the F.A.A. What it did mostly was reach out with the government's hand to investigate accidents that impacted transportation, from plane crashes to train crashes and everything in between. Anything that they had jurisdiction for, they investigated. The N.T.S.B. had gone through staff and leadership with an extremely high attrition rate due to the fact that the agency and its investigators were understaffed and the number of accidents that they were investigating grew exponentially each year. They were under budget and underpaid and it was no wonder they lost people. Since the Taggart accident had led to only one death, although an important one, the accident did not warrant a team of investigators. The investigator assigned to the case had simply had the recorder analyzed, had examined the engines and the plane's structural components and had determined that there had been no mechanical failure. The report had been turned over to Nickels who had reviewed the findings, personally examined the black box readings and had approved the report.

There were more than one hundred and twenty-five airline accidents that had occurred in the last 20 years from commuter flights to passenger planes that involved fatalities and the N.T.S.B. investigated them all, including Senator Taggart's plane crash. Of those hundred plus accidents, some were big, like the TWA 800 flight that exploded over Long Island, all the way to single engine plane accidents that apparently happened pretty frequently. Stories were told of investigators sleeping in sleeping bags in their offices and senior personnel having to order their people home from work. There was a tremendous amount of fatigue, which Matt could understand, but he kept wondering whether the investigators hadn't looked hard enough at his father's accident. He thought maybe they had come to their decision about his father too easily. Matt had made arrangements to meet with the Agency Director personally to discuss the case. Matt knew that he was only being given this meeting because his father had been a senator. Most families involved in accidents being reviewed by the N.T.S.B. only meet with the investigators.

When he arrived at the N.T.S.B. office, Matt was greeted by Amanda Silver, the investigator who was handling the case. She escorted him to a conference room a short walk down the hallway from the main waiting room. As they walked, she offered her condolences for his father.

"Thank you," was all that Matt said.

Ms. Silver looked to be in her late 30's, with an athletic build. She had long, dark hair pulled back in a ponytail. She had an attractive, yet strong face. She was wearing a black pant suit that, Matt observed, was tight in all the right places. Matt found himself looking at her, actually more like staring.

She placed a large file folder marked Taggart on the conference room table and offered Matt a seat at the table.

"Can I get you anything Mr. Taggart?" she asked.

"Call me Matt," he said.

She responded. "Okay Matt, how about something to drink?"

"I'm fine, thank you," he replied.

She then began pulling documents and photographs from the file. She walked across the room to get her computer from another table and Matt watched how she moved. She caught him looking at her as she turned around. She smiled.

Matt quickly turned his head toward the files that had been left on the table.

She leaned on the table and said "Director Nickels wants us to wait for him before we get started."

"That's fine," Matt said. When he spoke to her, he was looking away so as to avoid giving her too much attention. After some awkward seconds Nickels walked in the room.

"Mr. Taggart, I'm Leonard Nickels. It's a pleasure to meet you. I'm sorry that we have to meet under these circumstances."

"Thank you for making the time Mr. Nickels," Matt said.

"You're welcome." Nickels replied. "I'm just not sure you are going to like what we have to show you."

"I just want to know what happened." Matt said. "The truth, whether it's good or bad."

Silver then proceeded with handing Matt some of the documents. She began to explain to him the flight path, altitude record and air speed determinations, all derived from the black box flight recorder that had been retrieved immediately from the plane after it was located. She explained how the information is processed, how the parameters provided from the recorder are extracted and analyzed and finally translated into a computer generated re-enactment of the crash.

The investigator then turned her laptop that had been sitting on the conference room table toward Matt and began to show how they had reached their conclusion that the engine had been turned off manually, and that the plane had been placed in a nose dive configuration. The computer generated plane moved in slow motion as if it had rehearsed its moves accompanied by her voice many times before. She then explained why mechanical failure was ruled out based upon their finding that they could discover no failure of the engines. She added that the plane's radio was still operable and that no distress call had been made. She handed Matt a copy of the transcript of the conversations between the air traffic controllers and his father.

The report read that the flight CD475 departed the Washington airport at 0515 EDT bound for Charlotte. The flight contacted the air route traffic control center and reported climbing through an altitude of 12,000 feet. At 0622 EDT the controller instructed the plane to climb and maintain "FL 170." The pilot acknowledged by stating "one seven zero Charlie Delta." At 0646 EDT CD475 was issued instructions to change radio frequency and contact another air route traffic controller. CD475 acknowledged the frequency change. At 0702 EDT the controller instructed CD475 to go to FL150. The controller received no response from CD475. The controller called the flight five more times over the next seven minutes but received no response. The controller requested visual assistance from planes flying in that vector, but once the plane dropped off the radar, no visual sightings were provided. The plane was reported missing at that time.

The investigator and Director Nickels went on to explain that their goal was to determine the "probable cause" based on the evidence presented to them. Based upon the evidence presented, they had reached their conclusion that the plane was intentionally downed. They apologized again for their findings, but kept repeating that "they found no refuting evidence."

It seemed to Matt after awhile that further discussions weren't warranted, and he thanked the Director and Ms. Silver for their time and cooperation. He then left the building and walked the block and a half to the parking garage where he had left his car. As he walked, he could hear himself mutter out loud "why did he do it? Why did he kill himself?"

CHAPTER 24

After the meeting, Matt had called Linda from his car and told her what had happened. He told her he was just heading home. "I can't take the office right now," he said. Then he dialed in for his messages. He realized, as he listened to the messages, that Janine had done him a tremendous favor by picking up most of his messages and deleting the calls that were unimportant, passing along the case related messages to other attorneys and leaving only the personal messages from assorted friends and colleagues who were still calling to express their condolences. There was also a message from a man named Howard Goldman who left his number and said that he was doing a story about his father for The Washington Post.

When Matt got home there was a note that Linda had written down on the message pad that was located next to the phone in the kitchen. The note said "Howard Goldman," and had the same number. He decided he would call him back later after a long hot shower and a drink. He then decided that he would reverse the order and start with the drink, and headed for the refrigerator they had in the pantry that held the beer and wine. He picked up a Bass Ale and walked into the den toward his favorite leather chair and literally fell into it. The only reason he didn't spill the beer was that he was drinking it at the time.

He leaned over for the remote and turned on the TV. He intentionally skipped all the news shows with all the talking heads, since most of them were still talking about the crash and the suicide theory. He hated how they could talk about their opinions and suppositions about the crash without knowing the full story. He didn't even know the full story. It was always the same with them, he thought. Run the story that makes the news. They didn't even care about his father.

He tried to find a ball game on TV. Eventually, he got bored watching the Orioles lose to the Yankees and turned the TV back to the news in time to hear a Senate spokesman speak about Taggart the Senator, the impact of the loss, and how tragic it was to hear about the suicide. It was at this time that Matt actually started yelling at the TV, something like, "You're a bunch of assholes. You didn't even know him." Matthew wasn't sure what he was saying. He wanted them to stop more than anything.

He realized then that he had to do something, to tell someone who wanted to hear that it couldn't have been a suicide, or at least that there was more to the story about his father than just the way that he died, but more about the way that he lived. He walked back to the kitchen and pulled out Goldman's number and dialed it. Matt heard the man's voice on the other end of the line.

"Goldman," the voice said.

"It's Matthew Taggart. I'm returning your call."

"Mr. Taggart. Thanks for calling. The Post is going to run a story about your father and we're looking for the family perspective on why he may have killed himself."

"Mr. Goldman, I can tell you right now that we do not believe he killed himself. We believe, contrary to the N.T.S.B. report, that there must have been something wrong with the plane or some type of weather disturbance to cause the plane to crash. We do not believe he intentionally downed the plane."

"Mr. Taggart, I'm sorry to challenge you about that, but the N.T.S.B. report indicates that the black box from the plane shows without contravention that the plane was intentionally brought nose down for a crash. All the sequences confirm that the flaps and rudder were positioned for such a landing."

"You're right, Mr. Goldman. We can't explain the technical data. But my father was a happy man. He felt he was contributing something to his country. He was working on important legislation. He would not have stopped his efforts."

"What about the rumors we're hearing of poor health, marriage problems, financial problems," Mr. Goldman quickly interrupted.

"None of it true. All tabloid rumors. We've authorized a release of the autopsy to verify his health and we will be making a full financial disclosure. He had a blind trust that was doing quite well. My father had made his money in the market over the years and had made some good real estate investments in Charlotte. He didn't have money issues. As for his marriage, he was married over forty-six years to my mother."

Goldman interrupted again. "There are a lot of unanswered questions about the crash. Why does a plane go down when there is no evidence of foul play, weather in the area or mechanical failure? Unless we have something different, we have to go with the official ruling."

"Do what you have to do, Mr. Goldman, but this is not over. I intend to find out everything I can about this accident and why it happened. If it was an accident, I will clear my father's name concerning this suicide."

"Mr. Taggart . . . may I call you Matt?" Goldman asked.

"Sure," Matt responded.

"Matt, off the record, I knew your father while he was coming up the ranks on the Hill. He was a good congressman and a well-respected senator. He was a straight shooter. If you find anything to tell your side of the story, let me know. I'll get you the space you need to do it."

"Do you think you can help me?" Matt said.

"Matt, I'll do this for you. I'll try to do some digging to find out what I can about the plane and the N.T.S.B. investigation. If you find out anything, will you let me know?"

"Yes, I will," Matt said.

"Thanks for your time," Goldman said.

"You're welcome," Matt said, and then he hung up. It took a minute or so and the rest of the Bass Ale for Matt to figure out whether he had helped or hurt his cause. Either way, he felt better because he had the chance to defend his father's name and to blow off some steam in the process. He realized then that he had to follow up on what he had said. He had to find out why his father had committed suicide, and if not, why the plane went down.

Matt dropped his beer in the garbage, turned off the lights and walked up the stairs. As he reached the top stair he turned to the right and walked down the hall to look in on Sally, then closed her door and made his way into his bedroom. The lights were out. He could see the curve of Linda's body under the covers. She was asleep.

Matt walked as quietly as he could into their bathroom and closed the door behind him. He undressed, leaving only his boxers and grabbed a t-shirt from his closet. He threw some water on his face and leaned on the counter looking at himself in the mirror.

"Why did you do it Dad?" he heard himself say in a whisper.

He threw some more water on his face, turned off the bathroom light and walked to the bed. He tried as quietly and carefully as possible to pull back the covers to get into bed and moved quickly into his face down position to fall asleep. Linda moaned a bit as she rolled toward him and said in a sleepy voice "go to bed honey, it's late."

"I will, I will," he said.

Matt laid there and every time he closed his eyes all he could see was the computer generated image of the plane turning down toward the ground. It was making those rolls until it hit the water. Matt tried not to think about his father in the plane. How horrible it might have been for him. Matt just couldn't understand, couldn't comprehend what had happened. All he really knew is that his father was gone and Matt was determined to find out why.

CHAPTER 25

The next morning Matt sat at the breakfast table while Linda fed Sally her cereal. Matt drank a cup of coffee and read <u>The Washington Post</u>. Other then some discussions about why Sally loved Cheerios so much, Linda and Matt did not speak about the N.T.S.B. report or the additional stories that were in the paper about the suicide.

"I'm going over to my mother's this morning. I'm going to help her finish up her packing," Matt said.

"That's great honey," Linda said. "Is there anything I can do?"

"No thanks." Matt said.

Then he added. "I'm going to talk to her about Dad."

"Are you sure she can handle it?" She replied. "She's been through so much already."

"I need to know." Matt said.

"But maybe she's not ready to tell you." Linda shot back. "You have to think of her."

"I am thinking of her." Matt replied quickly. "We can't close this until we understand it."

"Matt," Linda turned and looked at him, "you won't be able to bring him back no matter what you find out."

Matt answered. "I know. But I have to try."

Matt took a last gulp of his lukewarm coffee, grabbed his coat and kissed Sally on the head. "Love you" Matt said to Linda.

"Love you too." She said. He kissed her and headed out the house.

As he made the drive to his mother's house, he thought about how he would handle the conversation. His parents had been married more than 46 years, had three children, an apparently happy relationship, but he needed to know more. He realized that any discussion about these issues would be extremely difficult, especially because Matt assumed that his mother had been asking the same questions herself as to how all this could have happened.

They sat in the kitchen around the breakfast table in a well lit bay window corner of the townhouse. The kitchen was full of flowers that had arrived over the last few weeks since the accident and the funeral. His question came somewhere between their discussion as to how Jenny was feeling and that his mother needed some time away. Then Matt spoke up. He said, "Mom, I hate to ask this, but why would Dad hurt himself?"

He could see the troubled look in her face, and her reply spoke volumes to him, part denial and part realization. "I don't understand, honey. I don't know why."

"Did he tell you anything?" Matt asked?

"I thought he was happy," she responded. "We talked about what would happen after the end of his term. He was considering not running again. We talked about traveling, spending more time with you and Linda and our grandchildren. We even joked about me becoming his golf partner. He wasn't sad. I just don't know what to tell you."

Matt hesitated before asking any other questions. He felt awful for asking, but Matt felt an emptiness in not knowing why. Matt began to think that all families probably went through this type of soul searching after a suicide, but the knot in his stomach told him that he hadn't yet even scratched the surface.

"Mom, was he depressed or anything? Was he taking any medications? Was he sick? Please, Mom, tell me what you know."

"I'm telling you the truth, Matt," she said, her tone a bit more stern. "I don't know why he did it. Maybe they're wrong. Maybe it was an accident. Have you thought about that?"

"They know what they're doing, Mom. You saw the report. He turned off the engine. I just want to know why."

"So do I, dear. Maybe you could talk to some people and try to understand."

Matt stood up from the table and leaned over and kissed his mother on her cheek. "I think I will, Mom. I think I will."

When Matt arrived at the office at 11:00, the first call he made was to his father's senate office to speak to his administrative assistant, David Wharton. He wanted to set up an appointment to meet him and talk about what had happened. When he reached him on the phone, Wharton expressed his condolences again and invited him to the office.

"Things are crazy here, Matt," Wharton said. "We have to keep things together until they get around to holding a special election."

"Do you have time this week?" Matt asked.

"Sure. Can you come by tomorrow at lunch? Let's meet here and we'll grab lunch in the Senate dining room."

"Sounds great. Thanks for your help, David."

That wouldn't be the only call that Matt had that morning. The messages were continuing to stack up no matter how many calls Janine diverted. Also sitting on Matt's desk was a pile of newspapers, including a full week's worth of The Washington Post. Matt realized that Goldman's article about his father had been published with what now appeared to be a page three large insert article about his father's life, his contributions to his district and the State of North Carolina and some articles about depression and suicide. Although Goldman hadn't quoted Matt from their phone conversation, he did reference conversations with the Senator's family, their disbelief concerning his death, and their verification that it had not been due to an illness. The preliminary autopsy report which had been provided to the press had also confirmed that Senator Taggart was not ill, notwithstanding some regular ailments for a man in his seventies. Since his war days Jason Taggart had kept in good shape and stuck to a regular exercise regime. The autopsy excluded any possibility that he had suffered a heart attack or even a stroke which led to any action on his part to down the plane. Matt thought the article left more questions than it did answers, but he was relieved that Goldman had left out any effort at scandalizing his death. Goldman also mentioned the plans under way to hold a special election to name Taggart's successor and efforts at restructuring the Senate committees and subcommittees that Senator Taggart had been involved with.

Matt was so involved in reading the article he didn't notice that Dwight Smith had walked into his office.

"Matt, where's the research on the medical defenses in the Tribucal case?" Smith's tone was demanding, not even a hint that he had any compassion left for Matt's recent ordeal.

"I don't know." Matt said. "Who was doing the work?" Matt asked.

"You were." Smith was getting red in the face. "You were sent a memo after you came back to the office. It's been a week at least."

"I never got the memo." Matt pleaded in his defense.

"Well I still need for you to do the work. Check the file. Get a copy of the memo from my secretary and get it done. I need it A.S.A.P. It's going to be a separate issue to try to block the production."

"What's happening with the documents?" Smith asked.

"Halfway done. About 50 boxes left."

"Finish it. I need to know where we stand." Smith said.

As he walked out the door Smith turned and said "I want the research by Friday."

Then he walked out of the room.

Matt pressed his intercom to Janine's desk.

"You hear that?" He asked her.

"Yes. I don't remember seeing the memo. I'll get a copy for you."

"Thanks." Matt said.

Matt took a deep breath and thought to himself "sometimes this job really sucks!"

CHAPTER 26

After working late that night to start the research that Smith had asked about, Matt got up early the next morning, knowing that he had to keep working on the research and also would be meeting with his father's assistant for lunch. He drove his car into the office about 6:30 a.m. to beat the traffic, get a good parking space and get in a few undisturbed hours before the phone started ringing. Linda had already reminded him about his pledge to work fewer hours. All that Matt could say in response was "I need a job. This is the only one I have right now."

He worked straight through the morning and left his office at 11:30 to take the Metro to the Capital station. After he exited the station, he approached the Dirksen Senate Building, presented his driver's license, and verified his appointment with David Wharton. David came out to meet him at the reception area and walked him back to the Senate office once run by his father. It was uncomfortable for Matt when he walked around his father's desk looking at the pictures of his family next to pictures of his father with the President and foreign dignitaries. It still did not make any sense to Matt that the accident had happened. Wharton first showed Matthew a pile of letters that they had received from constituents sending their condolences. As he scanned some of the letters, it became apparent to him how much his father had related to the voters and how much they appreciated his leadership.

"How are you?" Wharton asked.

"I'm okay," Matt responded. "Jenny really is taking it hard, especially with the baby being due. But she'll be okay."

"It just won't be the same around here without your father," Wharton added. "He had a way about him that inspired a lot of people. Some of our folks thought that one day he'd be president."

"My mother told me that he was thinking about retiring after this term was over, that he was ready to play golf and travel."

"You're kidding me," Wharton responded with a bit of a laugh. "He sure didn't mention it to me. And he certainly had a number of big items on his agenda. What do you think happened, Matt?"

"I really don't know," Matt responded. "I don't know what to think. But the flight recorder information seems to verify it was an intentional dive. Tell me something, David, what was he working on? Was he upset about things? Did he say anything to you about how he was feeling?"

"He really had been very busy. Certainly, there was a lot of stress in the office, but I think that's true with any of the senators. He had been working in committee on a few general legislative matters. His main committee was armed services, and he had been dealing with a number of defense bills along with the Pentagon."

"Anything in particular?" Matt asked.

"Not that I can think of," David answered.

Matt asked, "How about a diary or calendar or anything where he might put his personal notes?"

"I'm not sure. We've been packing up some of the office so we can look around."

Matt moved to his father's desk, pulled out the large leather chair and sat behind the desk. Initially he seemed to be lost in a trance as he sat in his father's chair, and looked out upon his office the same way his father had. Then Matt began pulling out the drawers of the desk looking through the notepads and small files to see if he could find anything that might give him some answers. His father had kept a pretty organized filing system. Many of those files were divided into policy issues, including notes from the Hill, as well as constituent letters. In his desk he even found a file of letters, pictures and notes that Matt had sent him over the years with a file tab labeled as "Matt." There were numerous files in his drawers, one dealing with his concerns over stem cell research and another dealing with a proposed state building in Charlotte expanding the federal judiciary offices. One file in particular carried a label typed as "F-20" that seemed to contain a number of spreadsheets, but no personal notes. Another file was named "ADX" which contained copied newspaper stories about a new fighter aircraft also named the F-20, apparently indicating that it had been designed for use in the Gulf War but never manufactured. The file also contained some Senate budget reports outlining cost proposals for the plane. Nothing seemed out of place and nothing rang any bells. Certainly there was nothing in any of the files he saw that would have led his father to commit suicide. Matt left the files and took a box that had been packed up containing some of his father's family photographs so he could bring it to his mother. Then he and David Wharton walked to the Senate dining room for their lunch. Their conversation during the meal was friendly and they discussed some of the more recent issues the Senator had been working on. The majority of their time was spent talking about what would happen to Wharton and the rest of the Senate staff who would likely lose their jobs after the office was closed. Some might be hired back depending on whether a republican was elected to replace Taggart.

After lunch, Matt thanked Wharton again for making time, wished him luck and made his way out of the Senate building carrying the box of photographs. Matt now considered the meeting with his mother and the Senate office staff as dead ends.

Matt stopped by the office on his way home from the Dirksen Building. He picked up his messages and opened some of the mail. He started organizing what would be his plan of attack for finishing the document review and the research that he was working on and also catching up on some of the other case work he had let slide over the past few weeks. He knew that the partners probably wouldn't continue to tolerate the continued loss of billable hours from someone at his level, no matter who his father was. He almost welcomed a return back to his normal life, even if it included being yelled at sometimes by Dwight Smith.

When he got home that night, Linda was waiting with a dinner she had made from one of her new cookbooks, which involved some sauce that had to be "reduced" which Matt still didn't understand but chose not to ask questions about. She had also opened a bottle of red wine, which Matt couldn't resist drinking at least two glasses worth. He wasn't much of a drinker, so the wine did its job of relaxing him fairly quickly, and put him in that tranquil place he had been searching for over the last few weeks since the accident. Sometimes he wished he could just get drunk and forget about everything that had happened. He realized at the same time that he had a baby upstairs that he still had to be responsible for. After dinner, Linda and Matt sat in front of the TV and watched some reruns of "Friends." He felt a bit selfish for being so comfortable, especially since he knew his mother was still in the townhouse, all alone. After the show was over, Matt and Linda walked upstairs and quietly opened Sally's bedroom door to take a peek at Sally sleeping in her crib. They both stood there looking at their daughter, both mesmerized by her peacefulness.

Matt whispered, "she's something special, isn't she?"

To which Linda softly responded, "she certainly is."

Matt stared at his daughter and then at his wife. "Sometimes I feel like I'm losing it," he said.

"What's wrong?" she asked.

"It's everything. My dad, my mom, work . . ."

"What about us?" she asked.

"You know I love you," he said.

"I love you too." She said. And then she kissed him.

Her kiss was warm and full and it brought Matt back to her. It was a connection to her that he had needed. Matt responded to the kiss and reached his arms around her and brought her closer to him. He felt stronger with her. They kissed more and then Linda turned and began to walk out of the room. She held his hand and led him to their bedroom where they fell on their bed and continued to kiss. It didn't take long until both had undressed and Matt had rolled above her. He kissed her gently on her mouth as they made love and repeated the words "I love you."

He stayed on top of her after they had finished. He withdrew slowly, kissed her on her breasts and laid his head on her stomach. She ran her fingers through his hair. "It will be okay," Linda whispered.

Matt closed his eyes and began to fall asleep. It was the only real sleep that he had gotten in days.

CHAPTER 27

The phone rang. Matt was always a pretty deep sleeper, except when it came to phones, creaky floors and Sally's coughs. He jumped up immediately and reached to pick up the phone that sat in the cradle next to his side of the bed. He looked at the clock, and the digital lights shone 3:30 a.m. His brain raced that any call after 10:00 p.m. was either a prank call or bad news. He reached for the phone and tried not to sound as if he was asleep when he picked it up.

"Hello?" Matt's voice was thick from sleep.

"Is this Matthew Taggart?" a man's voice asked.

"Yes. Yes. Who is this?" Matt answered.

The voice responded, "it wasn't suicide. He was killed."

"What? What," Matt said, "who is this? Who's calling?"

"They'll kill me for making this call."

"Who is this?" Matt was insistent.

"How much is it worth to you to find out what really happened?" the voice asked.

Matt hesitated. He was tired, but his senses were beginning to become very sharp at the reality of the conversation he was having.

"I'll need money to get away from them," the voice said.

"Money? You want money? Who are you?" Matt was now angry.

"I'll call you again." The line clicked off.

Matt's head was now spinning. Was this call a prank? Was it real? The man said that he wanted money. He told him his father's death was not a suicide. He sat there, not quite understanding what had just happened, and then turned and saw that Linda was awake and had also heard part of the conversation. "Matt, what's wrong?"

"This man just called. He said that it wasn't a suicide. He said Dad was killed."

"How? By who?" she asked.

"He wouldn't say. He says he needs money."

"Honey, it must have been a prank call. We need to change our phone number. Everyone knows that you were his son. It's just a prank call."

"I guess you're right," Matt said. He stood up and went to the bathroom, trying to shake the call off, trying to figure out now whether it was a dream or whether it really happened. What did the man say? He said he was killed? Matt couldn't remember the whole conversation. He remembered the part about the money, and the man also said that they would kill him. Why? What was going on?

Matt climbed back in bed and turned off the lights. Linda rolled over. Matt stared at the ceiling. Sure, he thought, like I'm going to be able to go back to sleep now.

What the hell was going on? Matt asked himself over and over. He repeated the phone call in his head a dozen more times. It took him another forty-five minutes to fall back asleep.

CHAPTER 28

The next morning, Matt was still thinking about the call, trying to understand what the significance would be of determining that it had not been a suicide and the ability to clear his father's name. When he got to the office that morning he called his brother to tell him about the call.

"Roger, it's Matt."

"Hey Matt, how are you?" his brother asked.

"Fine," Matt answered.

"How's Mom?" Roger hadn't seen his mother since the funeral.

"She's doing okay. I went to see her a few days ago."

"What's happening with the townhouse? Is she going to sell . . . . ?"

Matt interrupted. "Roger, I need to talk to you about something. Linda thinks it was a prank call, but someone called me last night. He said that Dad was killed."

"What? How?"

"He didn't say. He wanted money." Matt said

"Now that makes me think it's either a prank call or some type of set up," Roger said. "What else did the guy say?"

"He said his life was in danger. Then he hung up," Matt answered.

"I think I agree with Linda, especially since he was looking for money. Do you think he'll call back?" Roger inquired.

"Maybe," was all Matt could muster as a response.

"Then sit tight until he calls you back. Then let me know what he says."

"Okay. I will. Thanks for listening," Matt said.

"No problem brother. This thing has got me pretty rattled too. It's just weird without Dad around."

"I know. I'll call you if something happens, okay?"

"Okay. Give my love to Mom when you see her," Roger said.

"I will," Matt replied.

Matt hung up the phone. He felt a bit better after talking to Roger but the truth was that Matt thought the call was real. Either the guy was a great actor or he was really afraid, because he sounded afraid.

Matt worked the next two days full time on the Tribucal discovery research and when Friday afternoon came around he was able to leave the final version of the memo on Dwight's desk.

That night when he went to bed, Matt kept waiting for another call about his father, but it never came. He assured himself that Roger was right that it had been a prank call or some kind of money scam.

On Saturday, Matt chose not to go into the office and he spent the day with Linda and Sally, playing in the yard and working on his "Honey Do" list, including some repairs to the screened porch. That evening they went out with their best friends for a nice dinner at a restaurant in Georgetown, had a few drinks and tried to talk about things other than his father. When Matt went to bed that night, he had already forgotten about the call he had received earlier in the week. The phone rang at 1:00 a.m. in the morning.

"Hello?" Matt said in an irritated voice.

"I need a hundred thousand dollars," the man said.

"I don't have that sort of money. Are you crazy?"

"Your father did. Get it, and I'll tell you what you need to know."

"This is a scam. Leave us alone or I'll call the police." Matt's voice was shaking.

"This is not a joke. I know that your father was killed."

"Then tell me what you know and maybe I'll pay you." Matt was now baiting him.

"They will kill me for talking to you. I need to get out of town. I need money." The man was now begging.

"I'll get you help. I know people," Matt said.

"You don't know these people," the voice responded.

"What are you telling me?" Now Matt was hooked. He was pleading for information.

"It's about the flight recorder box," the man said.

"What? What are you talking about?" Matt pleaded again.

"I need the money tomorrow."

"Look, everything's tied up in the estate. I can't get that sort of money."

"What can you bring?"

"Look, I'm not bringing anything until we have a chance to talk. For all I know this is a gigantic scam."

"Okay. Look, if I can prove to you that it wasn't suicide, can you get the money?"

"Yes. I can always borrow the money if I need to. But I want to meet you," Matt said.

The voice responded, "it's too dangerous."

"Sorry," Matt said. "If you want me to help you, I need to meet you. Can you meet tomorrow? It's Sunday. How about in the city?"

"Okay." The man said. "Lafayette Park. The White House side. 12:00."

"Fine." Matt said. He was picturing the park and the White House in his head.

"I know what you look like Mr. Taggart," the voice said. And then the line went dead.

CHAPTER 29

Matt stood at the sidewalk of the park opposite the White House waiting for the man who claimed to know about his father's fate. Because money was involved, he started to convince himself that the whole thing was a setup, but he had to see it through, especially because the man had mentioned the recorder and the plane. It all seemed like a movie to Matt, some story that was happening to him that just couldn't be real.

But within a few minutes, Matt was looking down Pennsylvania Avenue at a man in a beige coat who was about a hundred feet away walking toward him. He was obviously nervous in his behavior, looking side to side as if he thought he was being followed. The man then saw Matt and his pace quickened to reach him. The man put on a crooked smile when he recognized Taggart. Then the man abruptly stopped at the corner of the street to wait for the traffic to pass. As the light changed, the man disappeared as a crowd as pedestrians crossed the street from the other direction and passed in front of him. As the crowd thinned, Matt saw the man again, but this time he was on his knees, holding his stomach. His smile was gone. His eyes were now wide with fear. Matt could see the man look to his midsection and then up again to Taggart. Then Taggart saw the blood.

The moment seemed to last forever, although it was actually seconds. Taggart ran across the street, to the man now down on his side, the blood turning his beige coat red. A crowd started to gather and Taggart yelled for someone to call 911. Matt reached down to the man. "Tell me your name," Matt asked. Air had escaped the man's lungs, and only short breaths remained.

"Tell me your name." Matt said again.

"Dean. Dean Saunders," the man responded.

"Were you telling me the truth about my father?"

The man replied with a shallow "yes."

Then man said "disc."

"Disc. What disc?" Matt was asking him. But there was no reply.

It had been only a minute, maybe two, before he was gone. The bullet in his stomach that blew out the hole in his back had taken most of his organs with it. The man had said a total of five words before he died. He had died because he knew something. Taggart also realized that he could not be found there with the body, or whoever had done this would know that he knew something as well. Did they know this man was going to meet with him? Were these people watching Matt now? Would they kill him next? He surveyed the people walking near him and next to him, his senses heightened. Matt knew that if they were going to kill him, he would be just as surprised as had Saunders. This wasn't a movie. This was real.

Matt ran back to his car. The whole time he kept looking behind him waiting for someone to appear or for a shot to ring out. Had they seen him? How did they know Saunders would be there? He turned the key and hardly waited for the engine to start before he pressed on the gas and pulled out from his parking spot.

During the entire drive home he kept looking in his rear view mirror. He was sweating. His heart was pumping a mile a minute.

This man had died in his arms, there was blood on his hands and on his sleeves. He kept reliving the words Saunders had spoken before he died. Something about a disc. What disc? Matt was talking to himself out loud. No answers came, but the sound made Matt feel good. It made him feel less alone.

As he drove up his driveway, he continued to have a feeling that someone was following him, watching him, waiting to kill him too. He immediately ran into the house, took a gulp of air when he saw Linda and Sally and realized that they were okay. He went to her. "Linda, something's happened."

"What? About the man you were meeting? What did he say?"

"He never had a chance to say anything. Someone killed him."

"What do you mean, someone killed him?"

"He was shot on the street right before I had a chance to talk to him."

"Oh my God. Did you call the police?"

"No, I got out of there right away."

"You have to call the police, Matt."

"I can't. Something is going on. I just don't know what it is." Matt walked quickly to their bedroom, took off his shirt and began to rinse the blood off in the bathroom sink.

Linda was behind him, she was starting to cry.

"Oh my God Matt, they killed him?"

"They must have . . . they must have known he was going to talk, either to me or somebody else."

"Who was he?" she asked, begging for an answer.

"He said his name was Dean Saunders. That's all he said . . . and something about a disc."

"What disc?" she asked.

"I don't know" Matt replied. "It all happened so fast."

"What are you going to do?"

"I don't know. I need to call Roger."

Matt sat on the edge of their bed and picked up the phone and called his brother at home. It was a Sunday. He usually was around on Sundays, doing stuff with the kids.

Marcia picked up the phone

"Marcia, it's Matt. Is Roger home?"

"Yes Matt, he is. You don't sound well. Is everything all right? Is it your mother?"

"No, she's fine. I just really need to speak to him."

"Hold on while I get him," his sister-in-law said.

A moment later Matt was describing to Roger what had just happened and Roger knew, along with Matt, that it wasn't a hoax. Someone was dead because they knew something. Roger and Matt discussed who they could talk to, whether it should be the police or, since Saunders had talked about the flight recorder, someone at the NTSB. They agreed they would start with the NTSB and Matt would follow up in the morning. At the same time they discussed if Matt was safe, if whoever had killed Saunders had known that he would be meeting with Matt. They decided that they must have known, that Saunders phone was likely tapped.

Matt finished his call with Roger and then moved to the other side of the bed to sit next to his wife. She had heard the conversation.

"Linda. I need you to take Sally and go to your mothers for a while."

"We're not leaving without you," She was quick to respond.

"I need to see this through. I can't do it if I think you or Sally could be in danger. Why not take Sally and go up to your Mom's? It will only be for a few days? Please call her now. I really want you to leave in the morning."

"If you really think so . . . ," Linda said. Matt was not happy that he had scared her.

"Linda. I love you. Everything will be okay. I just can't do this if I'm not sure that you and Sally are safe, okay?" Matt hugged his wife and kissed her on the cheek.

That night, while Linda was packing, Matt scoured the TV news stations for any mention of Dean Saunders or the shooting. A story appeared about a man killed in what police assumed had been a botched robbery or drug deal gone bad since the man still had in his possession his wallet and watch. The police did not suggest that it was a random killing on the streets of D.C. since the last thing they wanted was a public panic on their hands. The report said that witnesses on the scene did not recall seeing anything prior to the shooting and the police were asking for information to assist their investigation. At the time they said the man's name was being held until next of kin could be notified.

Matt didn't know what to do. He knew it wasn't a robbery or a drug deal, but he didn't know anything about the guy or why he had been shot. He decided to wait it out.

The next morning in Monday's Post there was a story listed in the Metro section about the shooting and identified the deceased as Dean Saunders from Silver Spring, Maryland. The article said that he was an employee of Bluestone Technology, located also in Bethesda. He was divorced with one child. The police were still asking for information about the murder. There was a picture of Saunders in the paper. It looked to be something like a driver's license photograph.

Matt walked into his guest room where he had his home computer and went on the internet to look up anything he could find on Bluestone Technology. He found the website on Bluestone. It described the company and the work it was doing in advanced engineering and listed some of its products under development. Nothing connected Bluestone or Saunders to his father or the plane crash.

After Matt loaded the luggage into Linda's car and said goodbye to his wife and daughter, he packed his briefcase with everything he had downloaded on Saunders and Bluestone and left for the office. During his drive he was wondering if he did the right thing by having Linda leave and he convinced himself that if he was overreacting, the worst that would happen would be the visit his wife would have to endure with her mother. His mother-in-law wasn't so bad. Matt had seen worse. The radio station was giving updated scores from the baseball games played last night and Matt was thinking about everything he would have to get done at the office, after he made his call to the NTSB.

CHAPTER 30

When Matt made it to the office, he immediately closed his office door and called Amanda Silver from the NTSB to talk to her about Saunders. Saunders had said his father's death had something to do with the flight recorder and had died for what he knew. Matt figured she would be the best person to talk with. The receptionist took his name and told him to hold in order to be connected to her office.

"Amanda Silver." She sounded curt but professional.

"Ms. Silver, it's Matthew Taggart."

"Yes, of course Mr. Taggart, how can I help you?" Her voice changed from heavy to light.

"I was wondering if I could talk to you a bit further about the accident?"

"Yes," she said. "How can I help you?" she asked.

"I was wondering if I could meet with you . . . out of your office. There's been a development I'd like to talk to you about."

There was now a hesitation in her voice, but then she said, "yes, that would be fine. Where do you want to meet?"

"Would lunch be okay? What about Houston's in Georgetown? Say on the early side . . . 11:30?"

"Today?" She asked.

"Yes, if that would be all right. It's quite important," Matt responded.

"I guess that would work. Okay. 11:30. Houston's," she said.

"Thank you Ms. Silver," Matt Said.

"Amanda, Please," she said.

"Amanda it is. I'll see you later. Thanks." Matt said.

The morning flew by, especially since Matt left at 11:00 to get to the restaurant even though from his office it was a 10 minute cab ride. He didn't want to be late.

He waited outside the restaurant and kept looking for the woman he had remembered from the NTSB office. He started to watch different women approach the restaurant and Matt became fixated on a woman who was wearing a low cut red blouse. And then, to Matt's embarrassment, the woman said. "Matt?"

"Amanda?" was his response. "I'm sorry. I didn't recognize you." This time her dark hair was not pulled back, but was down and laid across her shoulders.

"It's not always a suit day," was her reply.

"Nice to see you," Matt said. "Thanks for meeting me."

"My pleasure," she said. He opened the door for her and they went inside.

"I love it when you can beat the crowd here," She said. "I've never understood the wait but the food's always good."

"I haven't been here in ages." Matt said. "I went to Georgetown law. We used to come into Georgetown for the bars more then the restaurants."

"I love Georgetown," She replied. "I was happy to get the assignment here."

"Where were you before the NTSB?" Matt asked.

"If you can believe it, the Air Force," she said. "I learned about planes there. After I left, it seemed a natural step to learn about plane accidents."

"How long were you in the Air Force?" Matt asked.

"Four years," was her response.

"How long have you been with the NTSB?" Matt inquired.

"Five years," she said.

The hostess led them to their table and they sat at a four-top, Amanda choosing to sit next to Matt rather then across from him. She admittedly had been intrigued by his phone call and wasn't quite sure of the purpose of their lunch.

Matt popped her balloon when he said that he used to take his wife to Houston's when they were dating.

"How long have you been married?" Amanda asked.

"Three years," Matt answered. He restrained himself from saying anything about how his marriage was.

Amanda carried on with the conversation. "I got married during my second year in the Air Force. We were stationed in Southern California."

Matt looked at her left hand. There was no ring. He was sure he hadn't seen a ring before.

Amanda noticed his glance to her hand. "It only lasted a year," she said. "He's stationed in Germany now."

"I'm sorry," Matt said.

"It's for the best," she replied.

Matt changed the subject. "Let's order."

After they had ordered and the waiter left, Matt started the next stage of their conversation. Matt knew the minute that he began explaining his story about Saunders that he may have sounded a bit paranoid. In fact he told her as he was talking that he knew he sounded crazy.

"Amanda, I saw him shot. I think he was telling me the truth. It couldn't have been a coincidence."

"How can I help you?" She asked.

"I just wanted to try to figure out if there could be something that was missed. Saunders said my father was killed."

"You know Matt, we investigated the crash. There was an autopsy of your father. The findings are conclusive."

"What about the plane. Who found it?" Matt asked.

"Our N.T.S.B. dive team. It's S.O.P. for them."

"SOP?" Matt asked.

"Standard operating procedure," she answered.

"Is there any way I could talk to the diver who found the plane, just about what he saw?" Matt was getting a bit insistent.

"If you need to," she responded.

"What's his name?" Matt asked.

"We have a few special ops divers. I think the one that handled your Dad's plane was Derrick Tanner. He's ex-military. He's a good guy. I'm sure he would talk with you."

They talked further about the process of the underwater investigation of a plane crash. How the site is reviewed and what happens to the flight recorder, or "black box," after it's retrieved from the site. They talked about how the box is unsealed and the digital information converted into flight information. She explained how the data is analyzed based on other external factors such as flight control records and the salvage of the plane.

When Matt asked if the information in the black box could be tampered with, she told him that once the recorder was retrieved, the chain of custody was carefully maintained to preserve the evidence, just like any criminal case.

She tried to make Matt feel less paranoid about the Saunders matter. She suggested that maybe it was a drug shooting that had nothing to do with his Dad. But she wasn't too convincing. She finally agreed to double check the report.

"I guess that's all I can ask," Matt said.

When the check came, Matt paid it without any objection from Amanda.

They got up from the table and made their way out of the restaurant.

As they walked up "M" street Amanda said to Matt "I have to admit that when you called and asked me to meet you I wasn't sure if this was just business."

Matt was a bit embarrassed. He thought it was obvious that he found her attractive, because she was. "I didn't mean to mislead you. I didn't know who else I could talk to about this. I really need your help."

Then Matt added "I'm glad I got a chance to know you better." It was all Matt could think of saying.

Then Amanda kind of laughed and said "I seem to always meet married men. So, do you have any friends who aren't married who are as nice as you?"

Matt felt like he was blushing. And then he tried to joke it off. "None of them are as nice."

"Funny too," she said.

Amanda stopped on the sidewalk. "Mr. Taggart" she said as formally and as sarcastically as possible. "Thanks for lunch. I'll try to get you a meeting with our diver."

"I would really appreciate it," he said. "Can I get you a cab?" Matt asked.

"Nope. I'm gonna walk to the mall for a minute." She shook his hand. She held onto it for a bit longer then usual and then turned to walk down the street. Matt turned and walked in the other direction. About a half a block later he turned to see if she was still insight. When he didn't see her, he raised his hand to hail a cab.

When Matt got into his cab, he started thinking about what Amanda had said. He took a deep breath and took a minute to enjoy the compliment.

CHAPTER 31

When Matt got back to the office, Matt called his broker Stuart Stevens, asking him to do some financial digging on Bluestone Technology, hoping that Stuart could find some connection between Bluestone and his father. While he waited for Stuart to call back, Matt reviewed the faxes that had been left on his desk, some of the more pertinent e-mails and checked his voice mail. He then made his way back upstairs to the war room to finish his review of the Jamison documents.

It was about four thirty in the afternoon when Stuart called back and explained to Matt that Bluestone was a privately held company. Stuart had access to the corporate database that listed the officers and directors and some of the largest stockholders. Stuart agreed to fax Matt the list when Matt had asked to see it and within minutes the e-fax number allowed Matt to see the list on his screen. The individual names didn't mean much to Matt except for one, a board member named Max Wykert, the CEO of a company called ADX Aeronautics. He had seen that company somewhere. He just didn't know where.

Later that night, over a pizza and a beer at home, Matt continued to wrack his brain as to where he had seen the ADX reference connected to Bluestone. Had it been in the news? Was it something he saw at the office? Or was it in his dad's files? He fell asleep in front of the T.V.

When he awoke, he stripped off his slacks and dress shirt and climbed into bed. The house was so quiet. Matt felt very alone.

The next morning when he was back at work reviewing the Jamison documents, he decided to take a break and at least eliminate one possibility from his list concerning the ADX reference.

He picked up the phone and called David Wharton.

"Hello," the voice answered.

"David, hi. This is Matt Taggart. Sorry to bother you again."

"No problem Matt. What's going on?"

"Do you remember anything my father was working on involving a company called ADX?"

"Yeah, I do. It's something that he was working on through the armed services committee. There's been this fighter jet being pushed by a company called ADX Aeronautics. They're an aircraft manufacturing company and they are headquartered in Virginia. They've been around a while and claim this new plane is way ahead of the curve on military fighters. It's always been too expensive. Your dad had always been against the project because of the cost involved."

"Is that it?" Matt asked.

"Yeah, that's all I can remember. It didn't seem to be too big of an issue, although it's been on the table since '91 and the first Gulf War."

"Thanks, I appreciate it. Do you think that maybe I could get back into his office to look at those files?"

"Sure. Come by the office tomorrow. I'll put together what I can for you."

"Thanks, David. I'll try to get by in the afternoon."

That night at home Matt pulled out of his briefcase the information he had already downloaded about Dean Saunders and Bluestone. Then he logged onto his computer and the internet to do a white pages search on Dean Saunders of Silver Spring. He found his home address and phone number. Matt decided that after he met with Wharton he would take a drive out to Silver Spring to see where this guy lived and maybe to find out something about this disc. He went on Mapquest and got directions to Sauders' house.

.Matt decided that he would wrap up what he could in the office by 2:00, go to meet David Wharton and then drive his car out to Saunders' house to learn what he could about him. By one-thirty he had lost his concentration and decided to head out early.

When Matt made it to his father's office, it had been pretty well packed up by that point by the remaining office staff. All of the framed photographs and awards that covered his father's office walls had now been removed and boxed. All of his personal items had been removed. His space was being readied for the next senator who had the seniority for an office like his fathers.

After Matt arrived, Wharton had pulled out the file folders dealing with ADX Aeronautics and the F-20 fighter they had proposed. The file was about 3 inches thick and contained the proposed budget numbers, some notes concerning the committee analysis of the budgeting needs for the fighter and some articles that had been published concerning his father's position on the fighter and the history of its design and development. Matt thanked David for the file and promised to take him to lunch after David got settled in at his new job. David told him that he was going back to the other side of the Hill to work for a republican congressman from Colorado, David's home state.

Matt walked the files back to his car and took out the directions to Saunders place in Silver Spring. He headed out to the Beltway and went west. About 40 minutes later he reached Templeton Street, where Saunders lived. It was a townhouse community on a quiet street, with probably twenty homes, each connected to the other. He got out of his car and walked down the row of townhouses. Saunders' front door was on the right, another home to the left. The house seemed to be in good condition from the outside, with a recently mowed lawn, and a few pots of flowers on the front porch.

Matt wasn't sure what he was going to find, especially since Saunders was dead, but he approached the door anyway, hoping to find someone that Saunders knew inside. What he found instead was that the front door had been opened. He could see the crowbar marks against the doorframe. Matt carefully opened the door further and looked in. The place had been ripped to shreds. As Matt walked into the foyer which led to an open living room, it appeared that every piece of furniture had been turned over, cushions ripped, papers thrown on the floor. As he approached a small room off of the living room, which apparently had been used as an office, he found a smashed monitor, a keyboard, mouse, but no CPU. All remnants of any discs were gone as well. Anybody who was looking for information contained on that computer would find nothing. It was now all gone.

Matt carefully but quickly walked out of the house, closed the front door behind him and walked back down the street back to his parked car. Things were spiraling a bit out of control for Matt. Saunders was dead. Somebody was looking for something he had, and Matt was sure it must have been the disc that Saunders mentioned when he died.

He started his car and surveyed the street just to verify that no one had seen him go into the townhouse. His heart was racing. As he turned through the suburban streets to make his way back to the highway, all he could think about was how strange this all seemed. Matt needed to find out what was happening, but he also realized that he needed some help.

Instead of going home, Matt stopped at the Starbucks near his house, ordered a large latte and sat in the back of the store to review the files he had gotten from Wharton more closely. Matt began to read an interview that his father had given about the budget plans and his ongoing disapproval of the F-20 development. His father's opposition of the airplane was odd because his father had been in the navy and had always been a heavy supporter of the military. In fact, his support of the military had helped him win his first congressional seat and his assignment to the armed services committee. Yet this type of fighter project was clearly against his father's mind-set, and he apparently began to lobby extensively against the project.

There were also some articles about recent press announcements made by ADX which explained that the F-20 was in development and was the subject of review by the United States Congress for the potential purchase of over 100 planes. The numbers they talked about were in the range of ten billion dollars over the next five years. The articles mentioned that the Pentagon supported the F-20 project and quoted a Colonel Gerald Brier as saying, "once the F-20 comes off the assembly line, the United States Air Force will be unmatched in air offense and defense capabilities." Matt noticed in the papers that the Senate budget vote for the project had been scheduled for the week after his father would have returned from his trip to Charlotte. Matt wondered whether the vote could have gone through since his father had died. The information in the file didn't tell him much, but made him realize he had to keep digging.

As he pulled up his driveway and approached the garage Matt started thinking about what had happened to Saunders. If he had been involved in the death of his father and he had been killed, what would keep these people from killing Matt? Matt pressed the garage door opener and waited for it to fully open before he drove in. He proceeded slowly into the garage. He turned off the car, waited and then closed the garage door from inside his car. He never did that, usually waiting to close the door as he entered the house. But, he stared imagining that some sinister person would appear. His anxiety continued as he opened the door leading from his garage into his house.

CHAPTER 32

The next morning when Matt made it into the office there were a number of faxes waiting for him, along with numerous e-mails from other partners and clients waiting for his response to some ongoing matters. Matt couldn't help but be frustrated at the fact that the world kept spinning and work kept going on even though he was involved in what he believed was a much more important matter. He turned his attention away from ADX and his father to some of the more pressing matters that were waiting for him at his office, including another discovery issue that had come up in the Jamison dispute.

After about two hours of phone calls and e-mails, Matt decided to take a break. He walked from his office down the long hallway and poked his head into the office of Rick Davis, another senior associate that was coming up the ranks at Olimeyer. He and Matt were friendly to each other and sometimes found the time to grab lunch and complain about the firm.

Matt stuck his head into the open doorway. Rick had his head in some pleadings' files.

"Can I bounce something off you?" Matt asked.

"Sure," Rick said. "But make it a quick bounce. I've got Draper all over me for this motion." Draper was another partner, less obnoxious then Smith, but a close match.

"I'm trying to learn something about a proposed big budget plane that some company wants to sell to the U.S. Military. It was in front of the armed services committee, but it stalled there. I need to find out more about it then I can through just congressional channels."

"What about the Pentagon?" Rick asked. "If it's for the military, it has to run through the Pentagon."

"I wouldn't know where to start," Matt said.

"I have a law school friend that is with JAG. He works at the Pentagon. Maybe he can tell us something."

"That would be great. Can you call him?" Matt asked.

"You mean now?" Rick's tone was sarcastic at best.

"Yes." Matt said. "I really need the help."

"Who's the client?" Rick asked.

"It's more of a client . . . development matter," Matt answered, trying to avoid any discussion about his dad.

"Well if you land a fortune 500, you need to share the wealth."

"I hear you," Matt said, "but don't buy the Porshe yet!"

"Can you make the call?" Matt was a little insistent.

It took a few minutes for Rick to reach the right office through the main switchboard for the Pentagon, but eventually he found his friend. The guy's name was Jeff Stempler.

"Stempler," the voice said.

"Jeff? It's Rick Davis."

"Hey, Rick. How are you? It's been awhile. What's going on?"

"Not much. I'm at Olimeyer, Barkley & Smith. Been here since I left Meyer & Davidson. I'm doing corporate litigation."

"How's Annie?" Stempler asked.

"Wow. It has been awhile. She's gone. Packed her bags a year ago."

"Really. You still have her number?" Jeff was laughing.

"You're an asshole." Rick was laughing too. "How's Shirley?"

"She's great and Torry is already three years old."

"That's great. Send my hello's"

"I will." Jeff said.

"Hey. I've got a guy in my office, needs to impress a client. His name is Matt. Can he ask you a question?"

"Sure. I'll try to help."

"I'm gonna put you on speaker phone," Rick said.

"Hey Jeff . . . can you hear me?" Rick asked.

"Yes."

"Hi Jeff," Matt said, "thanks for helping out."

"What's the story Matt?" Jeff answered.

"I'm trying to find out the status of a pitch being made by a company called ADX to sell a fighter plane to the U.S. called the F-20. Ever hear of it?"

There was silence on the other end of the line.

"Hey, Matt, sorry. You're talking classified stuff. I can't talk to you about the progress of the project."

"Can you tell me anything about ADX?" Matt asked, hoping for anything.

"Not really Matt. I'd like to help you. But this is serious stuff. You have no access rights."

"Can you tell me about a guy at the Pentagon? His name is Gerald Brier."

"The reason I know about this project Matt is that I work government procurement. Colonel Brier is my boss." There was silence again on the line. "Hey Rick, I'm sorry I couldn't help. I gotta go," Stempler said.

"No sweat Jeff. Thanks for your help anyway," Rick replied.

There was a click. Matt looked up from the phone to Rick.

"Wow. You hit a hot button on him. That must be some uptight boss."

"Thanks for your help Rick. I hope I didn't cause any trouble." Matt replied.

"Don't worry about it. See ya' later." Rick turned back to his work.

Matt made his way back upstairs to keep working on the Jamison documents. Matt hadn't found anything to question Jamison's early testing of Tribucal and in fact, the files looked too clean. Through everything he read, Matt found nothing to indicate anything about anyone having any side effects from this drug, let alone dying from it. Although Matt hadn't done a lot of these cases, he had at least had expected to see something about some side effects. But there had been nothing.

CHAPTER 33

Matt's office was filled with files on the Jamison case. Not only was Matt dealing with the discovery issues, but he knew he would have to start the outlining for the depositions that would start to happen after the documents were produced. The case was starting to consume Matt, but he remained distracted by what had happened to Saunders and what he saw in his house. It bothered him that Saunders had worked at Bluestone, that the company was related somehow to ADX and that his dad was dealing with a potentially large ADX matter when he died. Matt knew there had to be some sort of connection, but right now he had nothing.

After about an hour of work, Matt put aside the Jamison file and went on line. He clicked on Google and typed in ADX. The internet then did its magic and the search generated 145 hits of references to ADX including articles about the company and information on its stock. Matt continued to search by scrolling down the list and picked the company website, ADX.com. The website was extremely colorful and undoubtedly was considered a masterpiece of website design. Not only was the reader able to click to company information, stock information and product information, but a click of the button allowed the visitor to experience the interactive adventure of entering the cockpit of each of their particular planes and to fly them, similar to the video games where the player can sit in the plane's jump seat and experience the sensation of flying a jet.

Matt surveyed the page and looked for information on the F-20. That page was under construction, stating only "we apologize for the inconvenience, but this portion of our site is not yet available."

Matt then did a Lexis search through the internet on pending budget issues before the Senate armed services committee. One of the line items included on the budget list, among about two hundred others, was the approval of the purchase of the F-20 planes. The information database also verified that the vote for the budget approval had been postponed due to the death of Senator Jason Taggart. Matt then researched information from <u>The New York Times</u> website concerning his father and his position on the armed services committee. From what he could gather, the next senator in line to be appointed to the committee was Senator John Frederick from North Dakota. It appeared to Matt that once Frederick was appointed to the committee the budget would be resubmitted, including the line item for the purchase of the F-20 planes.

Matt had to take a deep breath to take in the last few days including the phone call, the murder of Saunders and the questions which had now materialized in his own mind about his father's death. All he knew so far was that Saunders had worked for an aeronautical engineering company, said he knew something about his father's death and then had gotten killed. With the connection of ADX to his father, he needed to do more research on the whole F-20 project. He decided to try to meet with Gerald Brier.

He called the Pentagon and got connected to Brier's office. A lieutenant Baker answered the phone and took the message from Matt that he was the son of Senator Jason Taggart and wondered if the Colonel would allow him some time to meet with him.

Later that afternoon, the lieutenant called back.

"Colonel Brier has put you on his schedule for this Friday at 10:00 a.m. at his office. Will that work for you?"

"Yes Ma'am, thank you." Matt replied. Matt wrote the appointment down in his palm pilot.

About an hour later Amanda Silver called Matt and told him that Tanner had agreed to meet them to talk about the dive. Amanda reminded Matt that Tanner had told Amanda both during the initial investigation and then again when she had asked for this meeting that nothing unusual had happened during the dive. Still she convinced Tanner that Taggart was pressing her and he would only stop after he met with him. Tanner had reluctantly agreed.

Amanda told Matt that she would pick him up in front of his office building on the way out to Alexandria where Derrick lived. Tanner had agreed to meet them tomorrow after work, but did not want to meet at the NTSB office. He told them that they could meet at his apartment.

CHAPTER 34

Max Wykert, the Chairman and CEO for ADX Aeronautics sat in his high back leather chair behind a ten-foot long mahogany desk and looked out upon his office which measured more than forty feet in length and was surrounded by glass and steel. In front of him was a man that had once been military and now was a well-paid head of security. Before Max spoke, he pressed a small button at the side of his desk which created the "white noise" that he could use to discuss his important matters without the risk of eavesdropping devices listening to his conversation.

"Did you find the disc?" Wykert added

"We searched his house and everything at the office. We haven't found it yet," the man answered.

"It's unlikely that Saunders gave it to Taggart, or else he would already have gone to the authorities." Wykert said.

"Also we know that the NTSB has asked to meet again with Tanner."

"Wire tap?" Wykert asked.

"Yes sir," the man answered.

"Interesting," Wykert responded.

"What would you like me to do sir?" The man asked, already knowing the answer he would be getting. It was not the first time he had asked such a rhetorical question to Wykert. Wykert knew the attributes of this particular colleague.

"You know what to do." Wykert said. "No loose ends."

And then he added "and I want that disc."

The man smiled and turned toward the office door. Wykert leaned back, took a long puff on his lit cigar and exhaled slowly.

CHAPTER 35

Derrick Tanner knew the man outside his apartment door when the doorbell rang at 8:45 that night. He knew that man because it was the same man who had delivered to him the $200,000 for his work a hundred feet below the ocean floor. He did not know the reason the man had come back, although he knew that he could not prevent him from coming inside. The man who entered was tall and looked like a pro wrestler. Tanner always thought that he was in good shape, but this guy seemed almost twice his size. The man had a chiseled face and short cropped jet black hair. He had a scar that ran across his cheek. Tanner's stomach tightened as he let the man in. Tanner had never been told his name.

"What's wrong? Why are you here?" Tanner asked the man.

"There may have been a leak. We need to plug it," was the only response he got.

"I won't say anything." Tanner backed away from the man and continued to step backward into his apartment. "I have the money. I won't say a thing." Tanner didn't know that about an hour earlier, when the decision had been made, a withdrawal had been made from his account, erasing the previous deposit.

"We can't take a chance. Sorry." The man withdrew from a shoulder holster a black pistol, a 9 mm, and from his coat pocket a silencer.

Tanner stood there watching him as he screwed the silencer onto the barrel of the pistol. It was almost too late by the time Tanner understood that he was the target. He then looked around the room as if to plan his escape or what he could use for an attack. His mind raced, and he decided to make a run for it. He turned and ran toward the back of the apartment. At the same instant, the bigger man raised the pistol. The sound of the bullet entering the back of Tanner's skull was louder than the firing of the bullet from its chamber. Tanner's brain exploded as his body fell to the floor of his living room.

CHAPTER 36

Although Dwight had not asked Matt to follow up on any of the documents he might discover during his document review, Matt did find it interesting that there had already been some redactions to some of the documents, including some correspondence which Matt would later have to identify as "privileged" to avoid their disclosure. Usually, it was the lawyers who had made the redactions, so Matt assumed the decision to redact information had come from Jamison's inside counsel before it made it to OB&S for review. That was fine, but a bit awkward for Matt since he had to assume the redactions were properly privileged. Matt did find two letters concerning the results of some earlier trial tests of the Tribucal apparently conducted in Cleveland. The tests were apparently run through some local clinics where volunteers were paid to take the drug or a placebo and only the testers knew who had taken the drug. Parts of some of the letters and the carbon copies listed on the bottom of the letter were redacted which again Matt found curious, but he added the documents to the privileged list.

Surprisingly, about four boxes later, Matt found the same letters in another file. This time the "cc" was not redacted. The copies were addressed to a Dr. Charles Rosen. Matt could find nothing else on Dr. Rosen and then became more curious why his name would be crossed out on the other letters. It probably would not have phased him except for the fact that everyone else seemed to be accounted for. He called Jamison's assistant general counsel to ask for a follow up on who Rosen was. What made it worse for Matt was that the lawyer had called him back the same afternoon and told him that he doesn't show that a Doctor Rosen ever worked for the company and that he had not redacted anything in the documents that had been produced.

Now Matt didn't know who had redacted some of the documents or who Dr. Rosen was, but Matt wasn't yet motivated enough to take the next step to ask Dwight. He was only doing what Smith had asked him to do. The only thing was, since he wasn't finding anything, Matt was sure that he was not the first one who had gone through these documents.

At 5:30 Amanda picked up Matt as scheduled in front of his office. She was driving a red Honda, which looked as if it had already cleared 100,000 miles, but still had lots of miles left in it. She kept it spotless. As he got into the car and looked around, Amanda gave Matt a sideways look. Then she said "my Mazerati's in the shop."

"Hey, I didn't say a word," Matt smiled.

"At least it's red," Amanda added.

By avoiding the backup on Highway 40, they made their way to Alexandria in about thirty-five minutes. During the drive both Amanda and Matt stayed relatively quiet, all except some necessary small talk about the weather, last night's Orioles game and some background on Derrick Tanner.

"He's been with the NTSB for about four years if I remember correctly," she said. "He has been involved with a number of salvage operations as part of our investigations and he's a pretty good guy. Went through a bad divorce about a year or so ago. Story is, she took him for everything."

Moments later Amanda pulled up in front of Tanner's apartment building. It was a duplex and Tanner's front door was the one to the right.

Amanda climbed the three small stairs and knocked on the apartment door. Matt was behind her, waiting to be introduced. After a few more tries at the front door, Amanda walked to the front window and tried looking in through the window shades. She couldn't see anything.

"He said 5:30. He knew we were coming." She knocked again.

Amanda tried the front door, but it wouldn't open.

"I'm going to walk around the back. Maybe he's outside," she said.

She made her way around back and Matt followed her. She found the back door unlocked.

Amanda hesitated but opened the back door. She said "Derrick? It's Amanda Silver from the office." She tried again, this time stepping inside the backroom that led to the kitchen. She tried again, "Derrick?" But there was no answer.

Before she walked into the next room, she already smelled the stench. She yelled for Matt who was still waiting outside.

Matt ran in seconds later. It did not take him long to realize what had happened. He saw Amanda knelling beside the face down body.

The back of the man's head was gone. The wall in front of him was grey and brown.

Matt thought he was going to vomit, but nothing came out. He turned and walked quickly out the way he had come in, took a deep breath of clean air and then stepped down the back steps and sat down.

Amanda followed a minute later. She was already dialing 911.

Matt looked up at her and said quietly "What the hell is going on?"

She looked back at Matt as she spoke into the phone. "This is Amanda Silver of the NTSB. I need to report a shooting."

About an hour or so later the police were finished with their questions for Matt and Amanda. She drove back to the N.T.S.B. building so she could make her report to Director Nickels.

Matt waited for her in her office. He passed the time checking his voice mail and reading some recent editions of some aeronautical magazines.

Although it seemed longer, Amanda walked back into her office about forty minutes later.

The first thing she said was "I need a drink. Want to join me?"

"Absolutely," he said.

They ended up in Adams Morgan at a sushi restaurant and while Amanda drank Saki with her dinner, Matt downed two Japanese beers. Their conversation never waivered from the events of the day.

"What the hell is happening?" Matt asked.

"I'm as confused as you are, Matt. There must be something to this like you said. Whoever started this looks like they're trying to clean up the mess."

"But why Tanner? Does it have something to do with the flight recorder?"

"Director Nickels doesn't think so. He believes it's unrelated," she replied.

"Unrelated?" Matt shot back. "That's two dead guys in less then a week."

"Was my father killed too?" Matt asked, not really expecting an answer.

"I don't know anymore, Matt. I really don't. But we can't change the report until we know something conclusive. I'm sorry."

He mentioned to her his appointment with Colonel Brier.

"What do you know about the Pentagon's interest in the F-20's?" she asked.

"From what I read, they're in favor of it. Brier was quoted in something I read," Matt answered.

"What do you know about Brier?" she was helping Matt focus.

"Not much. Although I spoke to a guy who works with him."

Amanda recommended that Matt go back and talk with him again.

"Let's go." Matt said. "It's getting late." It was already after eleven o'clock.

They walked out to her car which was parked on the street about a block from the restaurant.

Matt said, "I'm gonna grab a cab back to my office. I have to pick up my car."

"No, Matt, I'll drive you there," she said. "You'll never get a cab now."

Matt looked around. The streets were quiet and Matt was hesitating about being alone anyway. He pictured Tanner's body in his head. "Okay, can you drop me back at my office?"

"Sure," she said.

Amanda and Matt got into her car and began the ride through town back to the downtown office.

Amanda kept looking in the rear view mirror along the way. She kept speeding up and slowing down the whole time with her eye on the mirror.

"What's wrong?" Matt asked

"I think we're being followed." Matt turned around and looked out the back window. All he saw were cars and their headlights behind him.

"How do you know?" he asked.

"I don't, but there seems to be one car that is still with me from the restaurant. Let's take a detour and see what happens."

Amanda turned right at the next light and Matt turned to watch to see if anyone followed. One car did.

"You're right." Matt said.

Amanda, without using her directional, turned quickly left. The car followed again.

"You're not going to your office tonight Matt."

"I agree. Where to?" Matt asked.

"I have an idea," Amanda said. "If it works, I can lose them on the way."

Amanda turned around and headed away from town toward the beltway. She took a number of turns and sped up to lose whatever car was behind her. Matt kept looking behind them.

"I don't see anyone," he said.

Amanda looked to her side mirror and then her rear view mirror.

"I hope you're right. Maybe they got the message."

Matt was nervous but impressed with her confidence and abilities. She made a final unexpected turn toward a condominium high-rise and drove down to the underground garage.

"Where are we?" Matt asked.

"My apartment," Amanda answered.

Matt was suddenly more concerned with the awkwardness of going to Amanda's apartment than with the perceived danger of the car following them.

She parked in her assigned spot. No cars followed.

After about a minute she turned to Matt and said "Are you okay?"

Matt hesitated. Again, he wasn't sure the question related to the recent car chase or the fact that she had brought him to her apartment. He answered "fine."

She got out of the car and Matt followed behind her. She led him to the garage entrance of the building.

He opened the glass door into the elevator lobby. She pressed 12 on the elevator panel.

"12th floor?" Matt said.

"Pretty good view, but it's not the penthouse," she answered.

The elevator door opened. Matt again followed her to her door.

She opened the door to her apartment and turned on the lights and gave Matt a quick tour which included the fact that it was a one bedroom. She told Matt to grab another beer if he wanted one and excused herself to go to the "ladies room."

Matt walked around the living room and looked at some of the family photographs that were framed and others that decorated the bookshelves that surrounded the television. He decided not to get a beer but instead sat down on the couch and turned on the television. He was half expecting to see some news story about Tanner, but there was nothing on about the murder.

A few moments later Amanda appeared, she had changed and was now wearing sweat pants and a Redskins t-shirt. She walked into her kitchen and took out two beers, opened them both and reappeared into the living room and sat down next to Matt and handed him a beer.

"Let's talk about some theories," she said.

She seemed oblivious to the fact that all Matt was currently thinking about was that he was in her apartment and that there was only one bed.

It was after two in the morning and another two beers before Matt made the comment that he thought it was probably safe and that he was going to call a cab.

Amanda said "I'd like you to stay."

Matt's response was, with a bit of a chuckle, "so what are the sleeping arrangements?"

Amanda leaned towards him and said "you tell me."

Matt looked at Amanda and hesitated, took a breath and said "this couch looks comfortable."

She responded "You sure?"

He looked at her again. Their eyes met. Then he said "yes."

With a sigh in her voice she said "I would really like you to stay Matt. I'd feel better knowing that you were here. Is that okay?"

"Sure Amanda." he said.

"I'll go get a blanket and pillow." she responded.

When she returned with the stuff to make up the couch she said "I understand Matt."

He took the blanket and sheet and said "thanks."

Then she playfully threw the pillow at his head and said "see ya' in the morning. Sleep well."

CHAPTER 37

The next morning, Amanda offered Matt some pancakes but Matt said that he would just take coffee. He told her that he wasn't hungry although the truth was simply that Matt wanted to leave her apartment as soon as possible. By the time Amanda had showered and gotten dressed, it was already after eight o'clock. When they left the apartment, Matt kept his head down as some of Amanda's neighbors said "good morning" as they passed in the hallway leading to the elevator.

Amanda stayed quiet, understanding that Matt felt out of place. She didn't quite get the "I'm married and I spent the night at your apartment" guilty feeling that Matt was experiencing. Nothing had happened, Amanda knew too well. That didn't change the fact that Matt was anxious that someone would see them and of course assume that he was having an affair. He just wanted to get out of there.

His speed at wanting to leave kind of hurt Amanda. She didn't know exactly why. Even though nothing had happened she didn't like the thought of men wanting to get out of her apartment like they had spent the night in prison.

She drove Matt back directly to his office. Although she still remained suspicious that they were being followed, she did not see anyone following them this morning. Nor did she see the tracer magnet that had been placed under her car during the night. She was being followed all right, just with technology. The van that was following them was at least six, sometimes eight cars behind her. They didn't need to follow as closely as they had done the night before.

Amanda dropped Matt in front of his office building. Although he was anxious that he would be seen with her, at least it wouldn't be at her apartment. He got out of the car and then leaned in through the open window of the passengers' door.

"Thanks for the excitement Ms. Silver," Matt said with a smile.

"Thanks for staying with me last night," Amanda replied. "I have to admit, I would have been scared to be alone after what happened to Derrick."

"We'll you're the world's best "let's lose 'em' driver" I've ever met. But then again, I've never been followed before," Matt said. Both of them laughed.

Amanda looked up, caught Matt looking at her and their eyes met. Amanda took a breath and said "I respect what you did last night. I just thought there was something there, that's all."

Matt was blushing. "Amanda . . . I gotta tell you, another time, another place . . ."

"So it's not that you're not attracted to me?" she interrupted, with a bit of a grin.

"Listen to me little lady," Matt used an impersonation of John Wayne to feign his anxiety from this conversation, "You're just lucky I didn't bust down that door last night."

Amanda laughed. "Really bad, Matt. But I appreciate it," she said.

"Amanda," Matt said with a serious tone, "will you help me figure this out?"

"Absolutely Matt," she answered.

"Thanks," he said. "I'll call you later."

Amanda joked back "sure, that's what they all say." Matt smiled, waved and walked to his building.

Instead of going into the office dressed in his clothes from yesterday, Matt chose to go directly to the garage and take his car home. Hoping he wouldn't see anyone, he jumped into his car and pulled out of the garage.

Along the way he felt good about the fact that nothing had happened, although it could have. Unfortunately, intermingled with his flashbacks from last night were the images of Tanner's body, the blood and brain on the walls and the maneuvering that Amanda had made to lose the car that had been following them.

Matt drove up to his house and rather then open the garage, he parked in the driveway and walked up to the front door. It was already opened. The lights were on and Matt was sure that he had left the lights off. Matt made the decision in a matter of seconds that he would go in rather then run away. He was hoping to either catch them in the act or see what they had already done. Everything in the foyer looked normal. Matt started walking toward the bedrooms. Then he saw it in the guest room. His computer was on and his desk was a mess, papers had been thrown everywhere.

They were here looking for the disc. He said to himself.

The phone rang. Matt jumped. Caller ID said "unknown caller."

Matt picked up the phone. He said "Yes?"

The voice said. "Do you have the disc?"

"What disc?" Matt said. "Who is this?" he asked.

"Don't play games Mr. Taggart. Lives are on the line," the voice said.

"I don't have it," Matt said.

"If you don't have it as you say, then stop looking for it," was the reply.

They hung up.

The phone rang again. Matt jumped.

"Yes?" Matt said in an angry tone.

"Matt. It's Linda. What's wrong?"

"Nothing. It's nothing. What's going on? Are you okay?"

"I called all last night. Where were you?" she asked.

Matt hesitated. "At the office." The last thing he was going to tell her was about Tanner and Amanda's apartment.

"I called there. I called your cell phone. You never picked up."

Matt did not respond. "Matt," she said, "I was so scared. I thought something had happened to you."

"I was just working on the Jamison case. I'm sorry. I left my cell phone on my desk. I didn't check for messages."

"You're not telling me something. What is happening?" She knew him too well.

He had to tell her, at least part of it.

"There was another murder." Matt began, "the diver who retrieved the flight recorder. He was shot." He left out the head part and the fact that he and Amanda had found the body.

"Oh my God. Matt. What are the police doing?" she sounded frightened.

"The NTSB and the police are investigating. It will all get figured out," Matt said in an effort to calm her down.

"You need to leave there, come here, stay with me here, "she was almost begging.

"No, not yet. It's close. Soon, I know it." Matt said.

"I love you," Linda said, "please be careful."

"Me too honey. Don't worry. How's Sally?"

"She's fine. She misses you too. Promise me you'll call me every day." Linda demanded

"Okay. I promise, I'll call you," Matt answered.

"Don't worry about anything. It will be okay," he added.

There was silence at the other end. "Bye," Matt said.

He waited for her to respond. "Please call me later," she asked.

"I will. I will" Matt replied. "Bye." He hung up.

He was spinning from both calls. The warning call and the lies he made to his wife. Although nothing had happened with Amanda, he didn't want to have to explain the situation to his wife. At least not right now.

CHAPTER 38

Matt jumped into the shower, made some coffee and then got dressed. He needed to get to the office and it was already 10:30. He decided he would clean up the mess that the visitors had made later and turned off all the lights again on his way out. He locked the front door and got into the car.

By the time he had gotten into the office Amanda had already left him via e-mail some information that she had learned about Dean Saunders. She told him he had worked for Bluestone Technology for the last five years, was divorced and his ex-wife and kid lived in Massachusetts. She listed all of his family members that lived near D.C. His mother lived in Virginia.

Matt closed his office door and then opened the files from his father's office that were given to him by David Wharton. From what he could tell with his research, ADX's contract for about 100 planes would total more than ten billion dollars over five years. ADX apparently had already lost money over the past decade on other failed plane projects. As the F-20 got delayed, ADX ventured into other aeronautical products such as satellites and rocket technology. But it looked to Matt that ADX was banking on the F-20 and continued to spend money on the plane with the expectation that the budget would pass.

Matt called Stuart Stevens again and this time asked him to look up anything her could about ADX Aeronautics. About two hours later, Matt received a fax from Stevens showing a ten-year graph of its stock price which only very recently had taken a move upward. In fact, the stock price had climbed seven points since his father had died.

Stevens had also found from his SEC research on the company that there had been a number of insider purchases over the last thirty days. The SEC required that they be given notice of such insider trading so that they could be a watch dog for potential violations. Matt saw that most of the money paid for the stock was from ADX's president, Max Wykert. The purchase of his recent shares alone totaled over fifteen million dollars. Stevens had put a handwritten note at the bottom of the fax which read "do you want to buy some? Do you know something I don't?" To which Matt laughed and said to himself, "I wish I knew more than I do."

Matt went on line and tried to find out as much as he could about Max Wykert and his history with the company. From what he found, Max was almost 80, was a former World War II fighter pilot and graduate of Harvard. He had this storybook resume of fine family breeding, Connecticut boarding schools, and then his acceptance to Harvard. His stint at Harvard was delayed briefly by the War, during which he received medals for heroics off of Islands like Okinawa and Iwo Jima. He had been injured when his plane was shot down off of Iwo Jima, but he was rescued before being captured. After his discharge from the service he returned to Harvard, finished with a degree in mathematics and made his way through the ranks of McDonald Douglas before he took a small contingent of engineers from the company and formed ADX Aeronautics. He started the business in 1965, before the Vietnam War had truly begun, before the Cambodian bombings and American troop escalation. By the time the war had been put in full gear, his company was already established and already had begun manufacturing defensive weapons for fighter planes, including counter missile technology. His company had made him a millionaire in less than a year.

The company apparently had another big buildup during the 80's with Reagan, but with the Democrats in office during the 90's, the contracts had been getting smaller and the layoffs greater, and he had been under pressure from a number of suppliers. It again appeared from what Matt had read that the F-20 was the plane that ADX needed to manufacture to survive.

CHAPTER 39

The next day, Matt had gotten into the office early. He wasn't sleeping well and not only did he have the death of Derrick Tanner on his mind, he couldn't stop thinking about the missing Dr. Rosen.

He walked down the hall to talk to Dwight Smith.

Smith was on the phone. He gestured to Matt to wait outside.

Matt walked out to the hallway and said to Dwight's secretary "Can you tell me when he hangs up?"

"Sure Matt," she said.

Matt loitered in the hallway for about five minutes when Dwight's secretary told Matt that he had hung up the phone.

Matt leaned his head in the doorway. "Dwight. Do you have a minute?" Matt asked.

"Yeah Matt, sure." Dwight responded.

"It's about the Jamison documents. I haven't found anything that challenges the clinical trials but," Matt added, "I did find something odd."

"What's that?" Dwight asked.

"There are some early references to a Dr. Rosen who worked on the trials. But his name has been redacted on some of the documents."

"It doesn't matter." Dwight said. "I didn't ask you to do anything besides review the documents and verify that there was nothing in the documents which would contradict Jamison's contention that there was nothing in the clinical trials which would have shown any danger to the drug. Did you do that?" Dwight's voice rose as he spoke.

"Yes." Matt replied.

"Are you done?" Dwight cross-examined Matt.

"Almost, just a few more." Matt answered the question.

"Okay. Let's just finish it," Dwight said.

"You need to follow up with Judge Lantham's office on the Motion to Compel. Once he rules we might be willing to turn over the documents with a confidentiality order," Smith added.

"I'll check on it." Matt said.

"Dammit." Matt said to himself. "We could have done that from the beginning. What a waste of time."

As he made his way back to his office, he decided to check one more time on Dr. Rosen.

He walked up to Janine's desk and handed her a piece of paper with his name.

"I want you to find this guy." He either worked for or consulted with Jamison. It would have been five to six years ago.

"And if I find him?" she asked.

"Just tell me." Matt said. "Not Dwight."

Matt went back into his office to keep working on the last few boxes.

The phone rang about an hour later.

"Matt Taggart," Matt answered.

"Matt, it's Amanda. I wanted to let you know something I've learned about Derrick Tanner. Before he was with the NTSB he was in the Army. He was stationed in North Carolina at Fort Bragg."

"So?" Matt asked. "Why is that important?"

"You mentioned that you were meeting with Colonel Brier. Well before he was at the Pentagon, Brier was the base commander at Bragg. The same time Tanner was there."

"Coincidence?" Matt asked.

"Maybe, but not the way things are going. I wanted to let you know."

"Thanks Amanda. I appreciate your help."

"No problem Matt. I'll make you repay me. I'll talk to you later. Bye."

"Bye" Matt said.

Now Matt was even more convinced than ever that he needed to talk to Stempler before the Brier meeting. He knew that Stempler probably wouldn't call him back so he decided instead to find Stempler. He went on line to find his home address. Stempler lived in Annandale, Virginia.

Matt drove into Stempler's neighborhood about 6:30 p.m. He parked across the street and called Stempler's home number. His wife answered and said that her husband was not home yet, but was expected soon. Matt said that he was calling on Pentagon business and would call back later.

Although Matt felt like he was in the middle of a stakeout he didn't have to wait to long until he saw a car drive up to the house. The garage door opened and the car drove in.

A few moments later, Matt was knocking at the front door. Jeff's wife, Shirley, appeared at the door. "May I help you?"

"Yes, hi. I'm Matt Taggart. I called earlier. I need to talk to your husband. It's a Pentagon matter."

She hesitated, especially because no one had come to their home before on a Pentagon matter. She asked Matt to wait outside until she got her husband. A moment later he was at the front door.

"Jeff. I'm Matt Taggart. I work with Rick Davis. We spoke on the phone."

"Yes. I remember. Like I said, I can't help you. You need to go."

"I know you said you couldn't talk about it, but this all involves my father's death. I need some information."

"Taggart. You're Jason Taggart's son?"

"Yes. I need your help. Can I talk to you about the F-20?" Matt felt himself pleading.

"Matt, I wish I could. But I could lose my job over this," he said.

"It will only take a minute. Please. I'm running out of options."

Stempler looked at Matt and then, realizing that Matt wouldn't likely go away otherwise said "Okay, but just for a minute. Come on in."

He called back to his wife who was now in another part of the house. "Shirley, I'm going to take Matt downstairs so we can talk."

"Sure, honey. That's fine," his wife called back from the kitchen.

Jeff then led Matt down to his finished basement which acted as a child's playroom and had a couch in front of a large screen television. "Sit down, Matt," Jeff said.

"Jeff, I'm sorry to bother you, but I need to ask you some questions about Colonel Brier and the F-20"

"What do you need to know?"

"First, there was this guy who was working at a company called Bluestone Technology. It's connected somehow with ADX Aeronautics. He called me and said that my father did not commit suicide."

"What did he tell you?"

"Nothing. Before we got a chance to talk, he was shot."

"Shot? How do you know that?" Jeff asked.

"I saw it. I was there."

"What do you know about ADX Aeronautics or Bluestone?" Matt asked.

Jeff replied "ADX has been working on this F-20 fighter for over ten years. Bluestone has been used as an outside consulting service for some of their projects."

"Projects?" Matt asked.

"Simulations of the plane, its flying capacities," Stempler answered.

"Have you ever heard of Dean Saunders? He worked at Bluestone," Matt said.

"No." Stempler answered.

"So, the plane," Matt asked, "why didn't the Air Force buy the plane?"

"Well," Jeff said, "it's expensive for one." Then he added "plus add a Democratic administration and a reduced military budget."

"So now, with Republicans?" Matt asked.

"My understanding is that the Senate appropriations committee had included it in the armed services budget, but it had not been approved yet."

"How is the Pentagon involved?" Matt was pushing.

"From what I can tell, there has been a lot of back slapping going on in the Pentagon with the ADX people, a lot of golf outings and dinner parties, especially with my boss, Colonel Brier who makes these purchasing recommendations to the armed services committee. I understand as well that ADX has been making millions of dollars in soft money contributions to various election campaigns to support the candidates who would support the growth of the military budget."

"Why would Brier care about whether the F-20 gets approved or not?" Matt asked.

"I'm not sure. But he seems intent on getting the plane built. He's been supporting the plane for awhile and has had some run ins with your father over the budget."

Stempler then reminded Matt again that the budget vote was scheduled last week to approve the planes, but "the vote got postponed." Stempler said.

"Because of my father's crash, I know." Matt interrupted.

Jeff continued. "I know that your father has for the last five years rejected the budget to approve the plane and was probably going to reject it this time as well." Just then Jeff's wife yelled down for her husband to help with his daughter.

"Sorry, Matt. I gotta go help."

I appreciate your time. I won't bother you again."

"I have to tell you, these appropriation issues are big deals in my office at the Pentagon. Please don't tell anyone you spoke to me."

"I won't," Matt replied.

After he left Jeff's house, Matt drove home to his empty house.

As he drove up to the house he watched carefully to see if any lights were on. There weren't.

He still hesitated as he pressed the garage door opener and turned the car up his driveway and into the garage.

"You're paranoid." Matt said to himself.

He walked in through the garage entrance into the house. He looked around. All seemed quiet. He walked through some different rooms and turned on the lights. The more lights he turned on the better he felt. Except for the shadows on the walls.

He opened the refrigerator, took out a beer and opened it over the kitchen sink. He then walked to the den and dropped into the leather recliner. He picked up the phone that was cradled next to the chair and began to dial his mother in law's number.

He heard her voice on the other end of the phone say "Hello."

"Phyllis, It's Matt. Is everyone okay?"

"Yes. Matt. They're fine. How are you? Linda said you thought they were in danger."

"I don't know what's going on." Matt said. "I just wanted to be more safe then sorry."

"Is Linda there?" Matt asked.

"She went out to do some grocery shopping. Do you want me to have her call you when she gets back?"

"No. That's fine. I just wanted to know that they were all right. Thanks Phyllis. Tell her I'll call her tomorrow."

"Take care Matt" his mother-in-law said.

"Thanks. Goodnight"

Matt dialed his office to check his messages. There was one from Eli who wanted to have lunch, a call from Amanda to wish Matt luck with his meeting with Brier and a message from Janine about Charles Rosen.

"There are a lot of Charles Rosens who are doctors." Janine said on the message. "I narrowed it down to ten who work in areas related to clinical research and women's health. That's the best I could do. They live from Michigan to Florida. There are only two in the D.C. area." Then she listed their phone numbers. Matt wrote them down and then said out loud to himself "tomorrow, we will find Dr. Rosen."

CHAPTER 40

The next morning Matt got dressed, made himself some eggs and coffee and left messages at the two numbers that Janine had given him for Dr. Rosen. His message was that he was an attorney and trying to locate a doctor who had ever worked for or consulted with Jamison. Then he had left his office number. At about 8:45 a.m. he drove directly to the Pentagon for his meeting with Brier. After he parked in the visitor's parking lot, he had to walk from the lot to the first of the security gates in the visitor's center. Matt presented his driver's license and announced his meeting with Colonel Brier. It was only 9:40 a.m., but Matt didn't want to be late. The private in the visitor's center picked up the phone to call in for visitor authorization to enter the building. Matt watched as the private listened to his instructions coming from the other end of the phone. Matt was then escorted to the desk which sat outside the office of Colonel Gerald Brier. The lieutenant who had scheduled the appointment welcomed Matt and asked him to take a seat since the Colonel was still in his earlier meeting.

Matt looked at his watch as it went past ten o'clock and worked its way to 10:25. Now Matt was waiting on Brier. Brier had the upper hand. It was his office and he controlled the meeting. Matt was starting to get nervous about his decision to meet with Brier, but he took a deep breath and again rehearsed what he was going to say. Then the office door opened and two men walked out of the office into the waiting area where Matt was sitting. Both men were military but one, he assumed Brier, had silver hair cropped in a marine type buzz cut.

The two men saluted each other and then the younger man turned to leave. The older of the two turned toward Matt. "Mr. Taggart I presume?" the man asked.

"Yes." Matt rose to shake the man's hand.

"Come on in. Sorry for the delay. It's a busy time around here. We're still having problems cleaning up the mess in Iraq."

"Yes sir," was all Matt could muster in response. He surveyed the Colonel's office. The walls were covered in plaques, framed medals and pictures. Behind Brier's desk were two crossed swords and a framed United States flag, tattered from bullet holes. Brier sat behind his desk. Matt took a seat in one of the chairs in front of the desk.

"I knew your father." Brier started off. "We met a number of times as part of the Armed Services Committee. He was a vet. He was a team player."

"But if I understand it sir, he was not in favor of the F-20 contract." Matt jumped out of the gate, primarily looking for a reaction. He got none.

"Yes, he was starting to be a pencil pusher on that one. But he was also starting to come around."

"I understand from his administrative staff that he was going to vote no again on the F-20 planes." Matt was looking for a response.

"Well, is that right? Hadn't heard that. Our sources said he had come around. Well, I guess it's a non-issue now." Brier said.

"What do you mean?" Matt asked.

"He's gone son. His vote doesn't matter anymore, does it?" The tone was sarcastic and hurtful.

Then the Colonel added "Can't apologize for a man who takes his own life. Can you?"

"What do you know about Max Wykert?" Matt asked. He was now on the offensive.

"Son, I was happy to meet with you out of deference to your father. But where are you heading on all of this?" Brier stood from his chair and was walking toward Matt.

"How about Bluestone Technology?" was Matt's response.

"I'm not familiar with Bluestone." The Colonel replied.

"What about a man named Dean Saunders?" Matt was pushing.

"Mr. Taggart. I'm running late. I'm sorry I couldn't help you. Lieutenant Baker will escort you out." Brier opened his office door inviting Matt to follow his lead.

"Colonel." Matt stepped forward and this time looked Brier straight in the eyes. "Do you know a man named Derrick Tanner?"

Brier turned his eyes back at Matt.

"Son. I suggest that you play detective somewhere else. You're wasting my time today."

Brier's face was red.

"I guess that means you're saying you didn't know Mr. Tanner?" Matt was quick to re-direct.

"What I'm saying is that it's a tragedy that your father killed himself. Seems to me though that it's best you move on and just worry about you and your family."

Was that a threat or a sermon? Matt wondered to himself. Either way, it pissed Matt off.

"Have a nice day Mr. Taggart." Brier shut the door behind Matt.

Matt left the visitor's office with Lieutenant Baker's assistance and walked out of the Pentagon building and back to his car. He knew as he drove away that he had hit on something with Brier. All the information was circling in Matt's head, ADX, the F-20, the Pentagon. There must be some connection between all of these that somehow tied into his father. Matt was in a dream world as he drove, questions buzzing in his head. He didn't even see the stop sign as he passed through it. He only heard the loud honking of the two cars that had almost managed to hit him.

CHAPTER 41

Due to the death of Jason Taggart, the senate armed services committee held their budget vote in abeyance until the committee could appoint a new member to the committee. Considering the Republican control of the Senate and the prestige of the Armed Services Committee, the appointment by the Senate majority leader was one that required a number of meetings with the President and other senate leaders. All parties involved wanted someone who would follow the President's agenda. As the media has guessed, John Frederick of North Dakota was appointed. He was considered a hawk and was consistently seeking to develop military projects in his home state. His constituents needed the jobs.

Once the appointment was completed, the committee had already rescheduled the vote on budget appropriations for the following Wednesday, which was only five days away. Assuming the budget vote passed, contracts would be signed within the next month and the conveyors would begin to roll within a few short months after that. The F-20 would get built, and Max Wykert and his company would be rich.

Matt called Amanda to tell her about his meeting with Brier and to find out if she had learned anything more.

"Not really," Amanda said, in response to the phone call. "This Saunders guy was pretty much a loner after his divorce. He worked. He came home. We can't seem to find any other evidence of other friends or acquaintances."

"Any other family?" Matt asked.

"Yes. His mother lives about two hours away in Southern Virginia. A town called Springhill."

"Do you have an address and a phone number?"

"Yeah, give me a minute. I have it here somewhere." Matt listened as Amanda put down the phone and then could hear footsteps walking away and then returning back toward the phone. Amanda picked it up again.

"Okay. Her name is Judy Saunders. She lives at 1143 White Oak Way, Springhill, Virginia."

"How about a phone?"

"Yeah, here it is. 703-558-2399."

"Thanks. If I find out anything from here, I'll let you know."

"I'll keep looking" Amanda said, "although I'm not sure if I'm just hitting dead ends."

"I know what you mean," Matt said.

After hanging up with Amanda, Matt immediately dialed the number that he had been given. A woman's voice answered on the other end.

"Hello?" the woman said.

"Yes, hi. Is this Judy Saunders?"

"Yes, it is. May I help you?"

"I'm calling about your son Dean."

"Yes . . . who is this?"

"My name is Matt. You don't know me, but I knew your son. I'm sorry for your loss. Do you mind if I ask you a question about him?"

"Were you a friend of Dean's? Oh, I miss him so badly. What a horrible crime! I hope they find the people that did this to him. The police told me it might have been drug addicts on the street."

"Ms. Saunders, he was coming to see me."

"He was coming to see you when he was shot?"

"Yes."

"Did you see him? Were you there when he got shot?"

"No," he said. Matt lied. He didn't want to tell her what he had seen.

"He never showed up for our meeting."

"I miss him so much. He was such a good son."

"When did you last see him, Mrs. Saunders?"

"A few weeks ago. He came to visit me. It was my birthday."

"Did he say anything about his company? Bluestone? Or a company called ADX Aeronautics?"

"No, he said work was fine."

"Do you remember if he said anything about Senator Taggart?"

"Who?"

"Senator Taggart. From North Carolina. The man who died in the plane crash."

"No, no. I don't recall anything about that, either . . . . What did you say your name was again?"

"Matt. Matt Taggart."

"Were you related to the senator?"

"Yes, he was my father."

"Oh my goodness. You've lost someone, too, haven't you?"

"Yes, ma'am, I have."

"I'm so sorry," the woman said. "Death touches all of us."

"Yes, ma'am, it does." Then Matt added "Do you mind if I come to visit you and talk about Dean?"

"No, no. Not at all. I'd like the company."

"May I come see you tomorrow?"

"Yes. Yes. I'll be here all day."

"Okay, ma'am. I'll probably be there about three to four o'clock."

"I'll make you something to eat."

"That sounds wonderful. Thank you again. I'll see you tomorrow."

"You take care now." She said.

"Yes, thank you ma'am."

Matt hung up.

He next called in for his messages. Nothing from the two Charles Rosens in D.C.

He called Janine and asked her to call the other eight doctors who were living outside of the city. Matt said "Don't tell them what it's about. Just ask them if they ever worked for or consulted with Jamison. That's all I need to know."

CHAPTER 42

Matt finished re-reading the discovery responses Jamison had provided in order to reply to Davidson's third set of interrogatory requests. Due to the delay in getting Jamison's documents, Davidson had filled up the time by preparing more and more detailed questions about the development and testing of Tribucal for which Jamison had to provide detailed answers, including another hundred or so "Request for Admissions" which included questions like "Admit that Jamison failed to provide all of its clinical test results for the drug Tribucal to the Food and Drug Administration as part of its drug permitting process." Jamison had denied that request. Matt had no reason to doubt their answer. If they had admitted the question, the case would have been over. Certainly, he believed, they would not lie about something as crucial as that. Even more, the CEO of the company would have to eventually verify the responses. If not as part of the written response, he would be asked those questions during his deposition as the company witness.

As Matt closed the binder and moved the inch and a half package of responses toward the back of his desk he pushed his chair away from his desk, leaned back into the leather chair so that his head fell back to the headrest and turned the chair on its spindle to look out the window that stood 26 stories into the air. Matt was lost in thought when there was a knock on his already opened door.

"Hey Matt. You taking your morning nap?"

"Hey Jack." Matt turned his chair back toward his office door. Jack was another senior associate at the firm. "I wish I was. This Jamison stuff is killing me." Matt said while shaking his head.

"You got lunch plans today?" Jack asked. "Rick and I are going to go over to Mad Hatters around 11:45."

"Thanks, but I can't." Matt said. "I'm already leaving early to meet a client this afternoon." Matt was lying about the client, but he wasn't about to tell Jack that he was going to meet Ms. Saunders.

"Yeah, sure," Jack responded sarcastically. "Don't hit too many into the water."

"Never do." Matt answered with a smile.

Once Jack left, Matt turned his chair once again to face his computer screen. He typed up "Mapquest.com" and inserted the information from his office to Ms. Saunders address in Springhill. The directions said one hour, ten minutes.

Matt left the office about three o'clock and made his way through the lobby to his car. Once he made all the right turns necessary to get onto 95 south, it was basically a cruise control ride.

Matt began thinking about what he was about to do. What would Saunders' mother know about what happened? Matt was convinced that he had missed something, something that would connect Bluestone or ADX Aeronautics to his father's plane. It was obvious to him that there must have been some kind of connection between Dean Saunders and his father. He knew something about the plane, and but for the bullet hole through his back he would be talking to Matt now. Nothing was left in his apartment, clearly gone through by the people who had killed him. Matt had to guess they were looking for the disc that Dean had spoken about when he died. They obviously hadn't found it or they wouldn't have threatened Matt about it.

The question was, where would Saunders hide it? He knew it was dangerous. He told Matt that they would try to kill him. The question Matt kept asking himself was how would Saunders have protected himself? Who would he have trusted the most? He apparently had no friends and it would be unlikely that he would have gotten his ex-wife involved. Matt was getting frustrated.

While he was on the road he talked to Janine and understood that she had reached five of the doctors who claimed they had never worked for Jamison. Matt had also heard back from one of the D.C. doctors who had left a similar answer, but offered for Matt to call him back if he had any follow up questions.

The drive to Springhill, Virginia was relatively easy. The Mapquest directions had gotten him there in about an hour. The directions took him straight to her house.

When he finally reached the neighborhood, he found her house among a group of small houses in an older section of the city. The area had fallen into disrepair, and the homes mostly contained elderly residents who had probably lived in these homes most of their lives. Saunders' house was a small three bedroom two story grey clapboard home with an old rusty screen door.

Matt only had to knock once and Mrs. Saunders came to the door quickly, happy to see a visitor. She immediately invited Matt into the living room, offered him some homemade sweet tea and some cookies she had baked earlier especially for his visit. Matt sat on the couch, and she sat in the chair across from him waiting to hear some words about her son.

All Matt said was "thank you for the cookies. They're delicious."

She began. "Tell me, Matt, how did you know Dean?"

"I met him because of the company he worked for, Bluestone Technology."

"Oh, yes. He loved working there. He was a very important man, did you know that? He told me he was working on some of their most important projects."

" . . . and when did you see him last?" Matt interrupted.

"He was here for my birthday. I made a wonderful dinner, and he brought me this beautiful plant." She gestured to some red-bowed greenery sitting in the middle of her dining room table. "He was such a thoughtful boy. We had a wonderful visit."

"Did he ever give you any documents or paperwork about the work that he was doing?"

"Oh never. No. He always said it was top secret, military things. Did you know that his father was in the military? He was a sergeant in the Korean War. Very handsome in his uniform. That's why I married him."

Matt talked with Dean's mother about Dean's studies at George Washington University where he received his engineering degree and his first job at General Electric out of college, leading to his later employment at Bluestone.

Mrs. Saunders then started talking about Dean's daughter and his ex-wife.

"It's been years since the divorce. They moved away right after that. I haven't seen or spoken to my granddaughter for years." She leaned over and showed Matt an old picture of a little blond haired girl no older then four.

"She's 13 this year." She said.

"Dean was buried here in Springhill. They didn't come to the funeral."

"I'm sorry Ms. Saunders." Matt said.

The conversation went on and the mother rehashed her son's relationship with his father and his problems with his ex-wife and how she still couldn't believe he was gone. She told Matt that she was all alone.

After an hour or so had passed Matt stood up and said "I apologize. I would love to talk longer, but I need to get going. I want to try to avoid the traffic heading back north."

She responded "Certainly dear, I understand. I hope you'll visit again."

"Yes Ma'am, I'll try" Matt said.

As Matt walked out of the house, and closed the door behind him, he continued his frustration of not understanding the connection between Dean's shooting and his father's plane. Once again, Matt had an hour to think about this during his drive home. It only gave him more time to think about what he had seen and what he had heard, and why none of it still made any sense.

Matt called in to check his messages again. His other D.C. doctor had called back and told him that he had the wrong guy. All but one of Janine's doctors had also responded. Matt figured that he would have to at least track down the one doctor that did not call back. This doctor lived in Tampa, Florida. Maybe there was a reason he wasn't calling back.

Matt then called his friend Eli.

The phone picked up on the third ring

"Eli Wheeler," was his response.

"I need a drink," Matt said.

"This is AA, can I help you?" his friend responded.

"I'm on my way back from Virginia. I'll get to downtown by 6:00. Can I buy you one?"

"Sure, but maybe two." Eli said.

"Thanks. How about 'Murphys'?" Matt suggested.

Eli said "Great, six o'clock. I'll see you then."

Matt looked forward to the drink. He pulled out a CD and popped it into his car player.

He listened to "The Best of Foreigner" all the way to D.C.

Matt parked on a surface lot next to the bar and walked in. Eli was waiting in a booth. There was already a pitcher of beer waiting on the table and Eli was drinking. Matt's glass was empty.

"Save some for me," Matt said.

"Early bird," Eli said. "So why the desperate need to damage your liver."

"I've got a lot going on buddy. You don't know the half of it," Matt said.

"So tell me. I've got no where to go tonight." Eli responded.

Matt replied "No date?"

"Nope. Off night. It's like working out, I have to rest up. One day on, one day off. You know how it is, right?"

"Don't make me kill you," Matt said. "I'm so tired of living vicariously off your love life."

"Did I tell you about the girl I met last week? Met her at "The Hideaway." She's a legislative assistant at some PAC for some type of saving the whales group." Eli said.

"What's her name?" Matt said.

"Who cares?" his friend answered.

"Oh, you are such marriage material," Matt laughed sarcastically.

"So, what's going on with your investigation on your Dad?"

Matt looked around to see who was around and then leaned in to talk to his friend.

"Eli, two people who are somehow connected with this have died. Both from being shot."

"Who was shot?" Eli asked. His focus now completely on Matt.

"First was an engineer that called me and told me that my Dad was killed, that it wasn't suicide," Eli's eyes got bigger. "And the other guy was one of the divers for the plane. We found him dead in his apartment."

"Who's we?" Eli asked.

Matt reacted to Eli's comment. "The NTSB investigator for my Dad's accident. She's been helping me."

"Helping you what?" Eli said. His tone was evident.

"It's not like that," he said. Then Matt hesitated.

"What," his friend said. "Spill it."

"Okay. But this remains quiet." Matt said. He looked straight at his friend.

"Banker-lawyer confidentiality," Eli replied.

"No such thing, but good effort," Matt said.

"All right, just tell me," his friend pressed.

"After we found the diver, we went back to her apartment. I spent the night."

"Oh my God," Eli said. "What happened?"

"Nothing happened. But she wanted to." Matt said.

"In your dreams," Eli said.

"It doesn't matter," Matt said. "Nothing happened."

"How about you?" Eli said. "Did you want something to happen?"

"I told her, another time, another place . . ."

"What a line, I'm going to use that later."

"Screw you," Matt said, taking the last gulp of his beer.

"Another pitcher," Eli asked.

"Sure," his friend said, "the truth is, I want you to help me try to figure out the connection between my Dad, this new plane and the pentagon. It's in front of me, but I can't see it."

"Well," Eli said, "Lay it out for me . . ."

And Matt started to tell Eli what he had so far. Eli took out a pen and used a cocktail napkin to draw circles for each of the groups that Matt mentioned. He started drawing lines between them. Then Eli said. "They all seem to connect to ADX."

CHAPTER 43

The budget vote was now four days away. As soon as Matt made it to the office he picked up the phone and called David Wharton, who was now working as a legislative assistant for a Colorado congressman.

"David, it's Matt Taggart. How are you?"

"Good, Matt. What can I do for you?"

"I need an update on the appropriations voting for the F-20."

"I don't know. I've lost track of the appropriations committee since I'm working in a different office. I can check on it for you and get back to you."

"That would be great. I need to figure out whether this F-20 is going to pass appropriations."

"Why the curiosity?" David put to Matt.

"I still think there's something connecting this ADX Aeronautics with my father. I just need to know a little more."

"Sure, Matt. I'll check for you. I'll give you a call back later today."

"Thanks, David. I appreciate your help."

At about four o'clock, Wharton called back and Matt picked up the phone.

"Matt, it looks like the vote is expected to be 5-4 for approval."

"Tell me something, David. If my father were still alive, how would he have voted?"

"I think it's pretty clear that he would have still been a 'no.' The vote had come up for procurement previously on the F-20 and each time he voted 'no'."

"So, wait. Who's voting differently now?" Matt asked.

"No one's actually voting differently. The new member of the committee, Senator Frederick from North Dakota, he's expected to be a 'yes.' He'll be the swing vote."

"Why is he supporting the bill?" Matt asked without hesitation.

"Well, one of the reasons is that he's been pushing for defense spending in his State. If he votes 'yes,' you might see some ADX manufacturing in North Dakota. He wants the jobs."

"Thanks, David. Thanks for the information."

It was pretty clear to Matt now that ADX must have had something to do with his father's death, since they had the most to gain from him dying. Once he was off the committee, the next person would vote yes and they would have what they needed for the contract. It all seemed pretty obvious. All Matt needed was some proof. He knew that right now, all he had was speculation.

CHAPTER 44

The next morning Matt got up and drove to the Dulles airport to fly to Tampa to find Dr. Rosen. He had the address that Janine had given him and he picked up the rental car at the airport. He found it funny that he was searching for Dr. Rosen the same way he was searching for answers about his father. These days all he had were questions. It left him with a lot of sleepless nights.

By the time he made it to the Rosen address it was 10:30 a.m., not too early, Matt figured, to make a house call. He parked in front of the condominium unit that backed up to the water and walked up to the directory. It was there. Rosen, 5B. He got into the elevator and waited patiently as the old elevator creaked its way to the top floor, the fifth. He got out of the elevator and turned right, walked past 5A and approached the front door of Rosen's unit. He rang the doorbell. A moment later he heard a woman's voice.

"Who is it?" She asked.

"My name is Matthew Taggart. I'm a lawyer from Washington, D.C. I'm here to speak to your husband." Matt needed to be honest. He was just doing his job.

Matt heard the chain go on and the door open. He saw the woman's face through the door opening.

"You're from where?" she asked.

189

"Washington, D.C. Is your husband home?"

"No. Not right now. He's downstairs, by the pool. Who did you say you worked for?"

"I'm a lawyer. How do I get to the pool?" Matt asked.

"It's in the back." She answered.

"Thank you. I'll find him."

Matt turned to walk away and the door closed behind him. He made his way back to the elevator and pressed "1". When the elevator opened, he made his way to the back of the building, through a metal gate and down a stone path until he saw the small community pool and deck chairs in the back. The pool area was empty except for a man sitting in a lounge chair reading the paper. His back was to Matt and he faced the waterway. He wore light khaki slacks and a blue golf shirt. He wore a dark blue Yankee's baseball cap.

"Dr. Rosen?" Matt asked.

"Yes. May I help you?" the man replied. He gave Matt the once-over.

"My name's Matt Taggart. My office called you. I'm an attorney for Jamison Pharmaceuticals."

"Who are you?" the man replied. He looked confused.

"I'm an attorney. I work for Jamison." Matt said again.

"So?" The man said. "What do they want now?"

Matt's heart started to pump a bit louder. He knew about Jamison. This was the guy.

"We're representing them in a case. They gave me your name to talk to." Matt was lying, but in a way, they did produce his name when they produced the documents.

"Then you know that they'll sue me if I talk to anyone about anything"

"Sue you?" Matt asked

"The confidentiality agreement. I've already gotten their damn certified letter."

"What letter Dr. Rosen? Who sent the letter?"

"I don't know. Some big shot law firm in Washington. Told me they would sue me if I talked to anyone. Damn lawyers." The man went back to reading his paper.

"I'm sorry Doctor Rosen. I haven't seen that letter."

"Then you should have done your homework. If I talk to anyone about the tests and what we found, I have to repay everything they paid me and then I have to pay them. They'll ruin me."

"I understand Dr. Rosen. I need to see the letter." Matt asked politely.

"Okay, okay. But then you'll leave me alone. Right?" Rosen was getting defensive.

"Yes sir." Matt answered.

Matt followed Rosen back up the stone path and accompanied him in the elevator as it cranked its way up to the top floor.

"You work for Jamison?" The doctor asked again.

"Yes I do." Matt said.

"The Cleveland study. Ask them about that. Ask them about the results and why they don't want me to talk. I used to think they were trying to help people. I worked there for forty years. I gave them everything I had. We were going to save people's lives."

The elevator door opened. The doctor walked out, Matt close behind. Matt's head was spinning. Was this guy for real?

"You're talking about Tribucal?" Matt had a tone of a cross examination.

"They've changed the name three times. But they can change it as many times as they want, the results won't change." The man responded.

He used his key to open the door and told Matt to wait outside.

"She doesn't like visitors." Rosen said. "I'll be right back."

Matt stood outside the door. It was probably already ninety degrees and one hundred percent humidity. Matt's shirt was soaked and he was perspiring from the heat and from the stress.

Rosen appeared at the door. "Here's your letter. Take it. Take it and go. You can go back and tell them I'll be good."

Matt looked at the letterhead. It was his firm. He looked to the signature. It was Dwight's.

"If they had just listened to me. None of this would have happened," Rosen said.

Matt knew not to ask anything more. He didn't have to. Smith would know it all.

"Thank you doctor." Matt looked directly at the man as he spoke.

Rosen shut the door.

Matt flew back to D.C. on the 2:00 p.m. flight. He couldn't get an earlier stand-by. He mulled around in the airport and called into the office. He didn't want to speak to Smith about his visit. He would confront him directly when he got back to town. On the flight Matt was given a center seat and was wedged between an overweight woman who stole his armrest and a traveling salesman who worked the whole time on his computer. Matt had bought the new Grisham novel at the newsstand while he waited for the flight. As the plane taxied for takeoff, Matt opened the book and began to read. He read through the entire flight only stopping to drink the coke handed him by the flight attendant.

CHAPTER 45

Matt had gotten back home by 6:30 p.m. He chose not to go into the office after he arrived at the airport, but instead decided to go home, reflecting on what he had learned and trying to calmly consider how he would approach it.

By 8:00 he had already defrosted and eaten his frozen chicken dinner and was working on his second beer. He sat down and turned on ESPN which was covering the Nationals home game against the Braves. The Nationals were already losing two to nothing and it was only the second inning. As Matt watched the game, he considered his options. He was tempted to immediately go into Dwight's office first thing in the morning and let him know what he discovered. Instead, he tried to consider all the different scenarios including the one where he got fired for flying to Tampa without permission to investigate something he was not asked to do. More importantly, now that Matt knew about Dwight's letter, Matt started to figure out that it was Dwight who had cleaned out the files and redacted documents before Matt had ever seen them. The confidentiality agreement and anything relating to Dr. Rosen and the Cleveland studies had been removed from the file. Davidson would never know. The enormity of the coverup burned at Matt. If he told Davidson about Rosen, it would be an ethical nightmare for Matt. Matt knew that he could lose his law license if he told Davidson. At the same time, he knew he couldn't participate in the cover-up, even if he didn't create it. Matt understood that if Davidson was able to learn about Rosen or the Cleveland studies a different way, then Matt would be clean.

Matt was murky on what resolution he came up with, but he decided to wait Dwight out to see what happened in response to the Motion to Compel. If Jamison won, it would all be a moot point. In fact the judge might limit the scope of the discovery to simply address the current question of whether the drug is safe now for its intended use as compared to allowing Davidson the opportunity of turning over every stone to determine whether Jamison ever knew, even early on, if there were potential deadly side effects to the drug on any particular class of patients. Matt decided to wait.

It was now the fifth inning. Matt had started his third beer. The score was seven to two. Matt would have no trouble falling asleep.

CHAPTER 46

Matt made it into the office about 10:30. He had slept in and intentionally had turned off his alarm clock.

Janine gave him a second look as he passed her desk and said "good morning."

"Good morning to you," she said in response. "Everything okay?" she asked.

"Fine." Matt chimed back.

Matt stewed in his office and tried to kill time and went about handling some smaller matters that had been on his desk for a while, one for Tom Barkley, and another small assignment for another junior partner. Before he knew it, most of the day had passed. He had eaten lunch at his desk. He once again declined an invitation from others in his office to join them for lunch. Matt recognized that eventually, they were going to stop asking.

Before the end of the day, Janine came into his office with a small watering pot.

"What the heck are you doing?" Matt asked, mostly in jest.

"Watering your plants," she replied. "At least I'm trying to," she added.

Matt got up from his chair and walked to the window where the plants that he had received as gestures of condolence from his co-workers were really looking shabby. He hadn't really noticed before.

"I started watering them when I noticed that no one else was." Janine said. "It is probably too late for this one," she pointed to the planter in the corner of the office. Matt walked over, inspected the plant and agreed with her assessment. He carried it over to his garbage can and turned the pot over to dump the plant. He thought he would save the pot. Maybe Linda could use it. He thought to himself that these plants really got a bad deal when they were given to him. He really had a black thumb. He took the empty pot and placed it next to his office door. He planned on taking it home with him when he left the office.

When he returned to his desk, Matt once again pulled out the manila file on his desk labeled ADX. It was the file pulled from his father's desk. As he looked again at the pictures of the F-20 he was re-running the events of the past few days in his head. He kept asking himself what he might be missing about Saunders, the disc and ADX. He decided he would take the file home and finish his review there. He packed his briefcase and walked out his office. He was two steps beyond the door when he stopped, walked back and leaned into his doorway to pick up the planter. The thought came to him somewhat subconsciously as if the possibility of the act was too obvious to see, but that by itself made it a clever ploy. Once he realized that he had made the connection, Matt returned the planter to the floor, dropped his briefcase and began running to his car.

CHAPTER 47

Matt pulled into Judy Saunders' driveway about an hour and a half later. The traffic getting out of D.C. at 5:00 in the afternoon was terrible. It took him forty-five minutes alone to get across the beltway to 95. He had called her from the road that he was coming, but it was only to leave a brief message on her answering machine. No one had answered the phone.

Matt's tires squealed as he hit the brakes in her driveway. Matt ran to her door and began knocking. There was no answer. He began picturing the worst, somehow envisioning Mrs. Saunders on the floor of her home with a bullet hole in the back of her head like he had found Derrick Tanner.

Matt began to run around the back of the house, banging on windows and doors with no answer. Suddenly a second story window above the back door was raised, and a voice said, "Who's there?"

The voice surprised Matt, since he was certain that she knew it was him and not some robber.

"Mrs. Saunders, it's me, Matt Taggart. Did you get my message?"

"Mr. Taggart? Is that you? Why are you here?"

"I left a message on your answering machine that I was coming," he called up to the second floor window.

"I'm sorry, I didn't hear the phone, I've been upstairs. Why are you here?"

"Mrs. Saunders, may I come in? I need to talk to you about Dean."

"Yes. Yes." She said. "I'll be down in a moment."

Matt waited impatiently by the front door. He was sure he was right. He had to be.

The woman opened the door. She wore a flowered robe. Her hair was in curlers.

Matt was abrupt. "I need to see the plant that Dean gave you."

"The plant?"

"The plant in the dining room. I need to look at it."

"All right. All right. Come in."

As she opened the door, he ran right to the dining room and breathed a sigh of relief as he saw the plant was still there. Flowers would have already died. Not a plant, though. She could have that forever.

He picked up the plant and looked at the base. It was a square ceramic pot. "I'm sorry, Mrs. Saunders. I need to see something."

Matt carried the plant to the kitchen, and turned the plant over in the sink. The soil came out of the planter, and Matt saw, packed in a clear baggie, a key, with a baggage tag attached to it. Matt opened the baggie and pulled out the key. He saw written on the tag the words "Sycamore Self Storage, Unit 1201."

"Matt, what is it? What did you find?" Ms. Saunders asked.

"Your son just left us a present, Mrs. Saunders. I think he just called us from his grave."

"What is it?" She asked. She seemed upset about the plant and about the fact that Dean had hidden something in it.

"I think it's the key to all of our questions. I'll let you know what I find." Matt kissed her on the cheek, and left out the door. He called back to her. "I'll call you. I'll call you." Then Matt said out loud to himself. "Mrs. Saunders, you had a very smart son."

CHAPTER 48

As Matt got in his car he started trying to assume whether the facility would be nearby Saunders' mother's house in Springhill or close to where Saunders lived in Maryland. He assumed that since he had left the key with his mother the facility would have to be nearby, and he would have stored whatever it was on his way to visit his mother. He picked up his cell phone and dialed 411, asked for directory assistance for Sycamore Self Storage in Springhill and received only one phone number.

When he called the facility, the answering machine said that they were closed for the night and would reopen for regular business hours at 9:00 a.m. the next morning. Matt decided to go directly there to see if he could find someone to let him in. The facility was an older facility, with a small two story building in front of a hundred or so one story garage door type units, and what appeared to be a separate building with some interior units. It was only a little after seven at night.

Matt looked in the office window, but it was dark. He noticed a lit window on the second floor. He began to ring the bell on the office door.

After about five minutes of continuous ringing, Matt noticed someone coming from inside the office. Matt then realized that the facility had resident managers who lived above the office.

A man of about sixty, maybe seventy unlocked the front office door, opened it slightly and tilted his head to talk to Matt.

"We're closed. Please come back tomorrow."

Matt was thinking on his toes. "It's an emergency." Matt said.

"What's wrong?" The man responded.

"In the unit. There is medicine." Matt said.

"For who?" The facility manager began to look around behind Matt.

"My brother-in-law has a unit here. He gave me the key. He has his medicine in the unit. I need to get it for him."

The manager looked at his watch. It wasn't too late he thought. He looked back at Matt. He didn't look like any sort of a threat.

"Okay." The man said as he opened the door. "What unit is it?"

"Unit 1201." Matt replied.

"What's his name?" the manager asked.

"Dean Saunders."

The manager moved to the computer terminal and pulled up his rent roll to find Dean and his unit number. "Yep. Its unit 1201. But I'm sorry. Your brother-in-law is delinquent on his rent. He's due to pay another month now. Payment was due three days ago."

"That's okay," Matt said. "I can take care of that. How much is that?"

"That's $52.00."

"Will you take a credit card?"

"Certainly will. I'll take anything as long as it pays the bills," the manager replied.

After the transaction was completed, the manager directed Matt to the location of the storage locker. The manager accompanied Matt since an overlock had already been placed on the unit due to Saunders' delinquency. He removed the overlock and then turned to Matt. "Do me a favor and get what you need so I can close up for the night."

"Yes I will." Matt said. "I'll be on my way in a minute."

"I hope your brother-in-law gets to feeling better," the man said as he walked back to the office.

"Thank you for your help." Matt replied.

The key fit easily into the lock and Matt removed the lock from the latch and opened the locker door. The storage locker was one of the smallest the facility had, about five feet by five feet, the size of a small utility closet. There was some old furniture in the unit, a table, some chairs and an old mattress. Under the table, Matt saw two cardboard boxes. Matt wasn't patient enough to simply take the boxes and look later. He began opening them. He looked around to make sure nobody was watching him.

The first box appeared to contain family photos and other personal records, including Saunders' college degrees and an old baseball trophy. Matt moved to the next box, which was where he found Saunders' will and life insurance policy and a brown envelope that contained a black computer disc and a single sheet of paper. It was the disc that Matt focused on, since Saunders fought to say the word before he died. Matt read the short type written note. He then quickly returned the boxes to the unit, put the disc and the sheet of paper in his pocket, locked the unit, and left the facility.

CHAPTER 49

As his car turned out of the facility driveway, Matt did not see the gray sedan parked across the street. His mind was racing as to what the disc contained and what it would tell him about his father. As Matt's car drove up the street, the grey sedan started its engine and followed, two cars behind. As he drove, Matt rehashed his late night conversations with Dean in his head, how desperate Saunders had sounded. Matt couldn't wait to see what was on the disc. He decided to drive straight back to his office to see what was on the disc.

Matt called Amanda on her cell phone but got only her voice-mail. He hung up and called her office. She wasn't there either so he asked for the operator to page her. Since the service paged accident investigators twenty-four hours a day, they were able to reach her with the message.

His cell phone rang about five minutes later. He recognized her phone number on the screen.

"Hello" Matt said. "Thanks for calling me back"

"What's up?" She asked.

"I have it. I have the disc. I found it at a self storage facility near Saunders' mother's house."

"Are you sure it's the same disc he was talking about?" she asked.

"There was a note with it." Matt said. "It was left for the police to find."

205

"Where are you going?" Amanda asked.

"To my office. I want to see what it says."

"I'll meet you there." Amanda responded. "How far away are you?"

"It'll take me about an hour to get into the city. I'll meet you there at about nine o'clock," Matt said.

"Perfect." She said. Then she added, "Matt, this is great. You're quite the investigator."

"You're a good influence," Matt laughed. He was feeling great, like he had turned the last piece to the Rubic's Cube. All he had to do was see what the disc said. He felt like the answer was right in front of him.

He said goodbye to Amanda and drove about ten minutes longer when the excitement was getting to him and he wanted to talk to someone else to share the news. The problem was, he didn't really know what the news was going to be. Why was Saunders killed? He had to know something. Saunders certainly would not have included the police in his game unless he was serious.

Matt pulled his cell phone out of his jacket and started to dial his mother-in-law's house to speak to Linda. The phone rang once and then he hung up. He had nothing to tell her yet. All he had was a disc. He hesitated. He had called Amanda, but was not ready to speak to Linda. He wasn't sure why, but he just wasn't ready.

As he was driving Matt thought about Saunders' decision to hide the key and the disc the way he did. It was smart thinking on Saunders part. If he stayed alive, he could always get the key to the unit later since his mother would take care of the plant. No one would find the key in his apartment. In fact, they didn't. If they killed him, eventually the self storage facility would inspect the unit and anyone looking through the box would find the note to the police. It was his insurance policy.

Matt pulled off of 95 and made the turns required to get to his office building. He had still not noticed the car behind him. Matt parked in the office garage, and ran to the lobby to find Amanda. The security guard had made her wait at the front desk since she did not have an ID badge to enter the building after hours. She ran to him.

"Matt, you did it." She said.

"Not yet," Matt countered. "We still need to see what's on the disc."

Matt showed the guard his badge, signed in and Matt and Amanda walked quickly to the elevator. As they got into the elevator, Matt handed her the note that Saunders had left with the disc. Her expression changed as she read the note.

It was type written. It read "To Whom it may concern: If you find this, please give it to the police. Tell them it's about Senator Jason Taggart's plane crash." The note was signed Dean Saunders.

When their elevator reached his floor, the opening doors made a "ping" sound and Matt led Amanda through the side door of the offices, using a key code entry that the firm had installed last year to avoid any more thefts of laptops that lawyers were leaving in their offices.

They immediately walked to his office and Matt sat down at his desk. He looked at the disc. It had a label that read "Bluestone." Matt noticed that it was the same handwriting that had been on the tag attached to the storage key. Matt placed the disc into the slot and waited for the computer to read the information. Amanda stood behind his desk chair, her hand on his shoulder. While he waited for the computer to read the disc, Matt realized that than the diplomas which still hung on the wall and the pictures of Linda and Sally that sat on his desk the office was unusually clean. Matt realized that his files had been removed. Obviously, the work had been reassigned.

He tried to open the disc first as a Word document, then as a spreadsheet, and then Amanda recognized the code on the icon as a type of pdf file, or a picture of a document, instead of the document itself. Matt had to go on the internet and downloaded the sample version of the software and, after unzipping the file, tried to open up the Saunders file.

When they first saw it, Matt couldn't decipher what he was looking at, he thought it looked like some type of computer program, but Amanda's reaction was different. She said "oh my God" slightly above a whisper and then asked Matt to get up so she could get a closer look.

As she moved the mouse around the screen, she explained that what they were looking at were the parameters for a flight data recorder which indicated altitude, air speed and heading. She explained that once a flight data recorder was recovered from an accident, its date is retrieved from the computer chip inside the box and displayed the way they were seeing it now. From this information, flight investigators can piece together what happened to the plane, similar to what Amanda had demonstrated to Matt on her laptop that day in her office with Director Nickels.

"So," Matt asked, "why is this flight data important?"

Amanda hesitated, looked again at one portion of the data and then turned to look upwards at Matt and replied.

"Because this information is identical to the flight parameters of your father's plane."

"So, couldn't he have created this from all the information given to the public about the crash?"

"Maybe, except that the information on this disc was formulated a month before your father's crash."

The information they read showed the same data which validated the N.T.S.B's findings that the pilot had intentionally shut down the engines and turned the plane for its death dive. What they were looking at was the information about the flight and the crash before the plane had ever left the ground.

"What does this all mean?" Matt said. "How could Saunders have a disc of what the flight recorder would say before the flight was even taken?"

"I don't know." Silver said. "It's as if Saunders had the schematics to build a flight recorder for the plane with the flight information prerecorded before the flight even took off. But that doesn't explain why the plane went down or why he didn't call for help." Amanda said.

Then Matt heard the soft ping of the elevator doors opening from down the hall. He looked at his watch and saw that it was after nine-thirty at night. At first he didn't think twice about it, considering that at this time of night the cleaning crew might still be in some of the offices, or there could certainly be another lawyer in the office working late, maybe having returned to the office having gone home for dinner, which was common for some of the other lawyers in the office. But then he realized that he had the disc.

He took Amanda's hand and said "we have to get out of here."

"Why?" Amanda shot back.

"I think it's them. They must have followed me or you." He pulled her from the chair and led her to his office door. Matt leaned his head out of the door enough to look down the hallway toward the front lobby of the office.

Then he heard another sound, a sound that made the hair on his neck shoot up, and he realized that the front lobby glass doors were opening. He turned to Amanda and said "we have to make it to the back door. We can go down the exit stairs." Matt looked again out the door, saw nothing and ran from his office holding Amanda's hand and leading her around the secretary's cubicles that he knew so well from working here all these years.

They reached the back hallway, where all the file drawers were located and Matt could see the fire escape door. It was then that Matt realized that they had left the disc in the computer.

"Take the stairs down to the lobby and get security to call the police. I'm going to go back and get the disc."

"No Matt, it's too dangerous." She was holding on to his arm. "Don't go."

"I have to. It's my evidence. It will clear my father's name. Now Go!" Matt said and he pushed her toward the exit door.

Matt crept back around the secretary's offices toward his office but before he could stand up, he heard the voice behind him.

"Get up," the voice said.

Matt did as he was told.

Then Matt felt a cold hard object come up against his left temple as the man moved slowly in front of him.

The man was huge, if not in height, then in mass. He looked like one of the characters from "Universal Soldier." He had a blank expression on his face, but at the same time some faint smirk, signifying that what he was doing was something he enjoyed the most about his work, the power of control over life and death.

As Matt looked at the man, his mind began to race about the possibility of escape. All he could picture was how Saunders and Tanner had died. Snippets of pictures, of the blood and the bodies all came into his mind, only to be interrupted with the words of the man who spoke.

"I want the disc."

"What disc?" Matt said. His faint effort at lying and evasion was useless.

The man raised his arm and Matt again saw the gun in his hand. "I'll say it one more time. I want the disc."

"I don't have it," Matt said.

"Where is it?"

Matt thought through the possibilities. Should he say Amanda has it? No, then the man could kill him and simply go after Amanda. He needed the disc to live.

"It's still in the computer room," Matt said. To which the man responded, "show me."

The question sounded easier than it was, since there really was no computer room in the office. Matt was only trying to find a way to buy some time.

Matt was trying to size the man up. He realized he was the same height as the man who stood in front of him, if not a bit taller, but clearly forty to fifty pounds lighter. He would not have a chance to overpower him, especially since the man had a gun. The man was making the same determination, about a potential matchup with Matt, recognizing that if he made a move, he would simply shoot him.

Matt realized he would have to run. They began to move down the hallway since Matt told him that the computer room was at the end of the hall. Matt started thinking about how he would escape, and how far he would have to get to avoid getting shot. He knew he had to try something. Otherwise, this man would certainly kill him. Matt was convinced that the man would enjoy it.

He approached a corner of the office which had been built as an architectural addition to the space. Behind that corner was a hallway which turned back off the main hall and led to an area behind the secretary bays to the copiers and scanners. Matt knew that if he could turn the corner fast enough, that by the time the man followed him,

Matt would already have turned the second corner so as to hopefully avoid a direct line of fire. After that he didn't have a plan.

Matt started walking a little faster, a bit noticeable to him, but hopefully indiscernible to his larger shadow since Matt already was walking a bit faster after the man had ordered him to move ahead. As he approached the corner, he turned his head to the left, pointed and said, "it's right up here," hoping that the man would at least let his guard up an instant since he was likely to accomplish his mission.

His man responded with the order, "move," which gave Matt the excuse to dart ahead and take the four or five steps which were necessary to get ahead of his unfriendly companion. He made his move and by the time his planned killer had turned the corner as well, Matt had already gotten around the angular second corner and toward the back room.

Then he heard the man say, "you're a dead man. You're wasting my time. Give me the disc now and I'll kill you quick. Make me find it and I'll make you suffer, you little shit."

Matt made his moves through the back office as quietly as he could, but realized that he had to get away if he was going to survive. Where was Amanda and the police? He needed time.

He decided he needed the benefit of darkness to avoid getting caught and somehow he would have to reach the electrical box for the office. He had seen it used before when repairs had been made to a short circuit and the lines had to be turned off for the repairs.

He found his way to the electrical closet and hit the main fuse to kill the lights. The sound was sharp and loud as the lights clicked off, and he heard the man scream loud, "it's going to be a pleasure to kill you, just like we killed your father." With the inside lights off and only moonlight coming in through the office windows, the hallways were dark.

Amanda was running down the twenty-six floors of the office building and had already kicked off her shoes with the three inch heels since she had already tripped once. She made it to the lobby and pushed open the large metal exit door which slammed against the lobby wall. She burst out of the doorway as if she had been underwater and she had finally made it to the surface. She screamed for help and looked back and forth for the security guard as she ran toward the lobby desk yelling "help, someone help us." But she saw nothing. It was only when she reached the security desk did she see the guard slumped back against his chair, a bullet hole in the center of his forehead and only a few coagulated drops of blood that had dripped across his open eyelids and onto his cheek.

Amanda froze at the sight, but then gathered herself and moved behind the security desk and picked up the phone dialing 911 as fast as she could. She didn't know if Matt had any time left.

Matt made his way back to his office like a blind man who once had sight. He knew what the firm's offices looked like and now, in the dark, he had to trace his steps back to his office to retrieve the disc by following along the hallway walls. When he reached his office he quietly removed the disc from the computer and started to retrace his earlier steps to the back entrance when the man once again spoke.

"You're not leaving here alive."

The man was guarding the back door exit where Amanda had made her escape and Matt realized he would have to find another way out.

Matt moved away from the sound of the man's voice and realized that he was heading back toward the far corner of the office. There was no exit.

As the man's voice became louder, Matt found himself walking back toward Dwight Smith's corner office. He was being trapped. He would have no choice but to fight back.

What weapon did he have? Matt asked himself. He felt around in Dwight's office. He found a letter opener, a bookend. What else? Then he remembered the golf putter resting in the corner of Smith's office. Smith had a putter and one of those electric ball return gadgets. Smith always said that he was practicing up for his sub par rounds, although Matt had only seen him use the putter once. Otherwise, it sat there getting dusty like a decorative item on a bookshelf.

There was enough moonlight that shone through Dwight's floor to ceiling windows in his corner office that Matt was able to find the putter.

He waited inside the office and started thinking about his status at the moment. "I am holding a putter and he has a gun. He's going to kill me." Matt felt like he was some guy who hears a burglar at night and grabs a shoe. "That will scare them away." Matt sarcastically thought to himself. But Matt knew that he had to get away from the man if he were to live.

Then he heard the voice outside in the hallway. The man was calling out, "Get out here, you little shit. You are dead. Let's get it over with. I want the disc now."

Matt knew he had no choice. He made his way to the door and looked down the hall. Even with little light, Matt could see a glint of steel from the gun as the soldier moved his way up the hall, bringing the gun up and down, back and forth, looking for his prey. Matt pulled the putter back like a baseball player waiting on a fastball and stood in his place waiting for what felt like an eternity until the steps came closer.

He knew he had no choice but to make the swing and hope for the best. He decided on aiming for the man's head, knowing that if he missed, he'd still have a chance to swing again, at least with the element of surprise. He felt the sweat build up on his forehead as he tried to measure the distance in his mind against the steps that he heard coming closer.

Then he did it. He stepped out from behind the door and swung the putter at the man's head. The assailant stood there for an instant, since he had not been looking to the left when Matt stepped out and truly had not been expecting any sort of attack from a guy who he thought might just be hiding under a desk somewhere.

The putter hit him in his left jaw, just enough to make him lose his balance to the right. By the time the man had raised his head again, Matt was already returning with his switch hitter swing. Matt was looking to connect for the long ball. This time, based upon the position of the man's head and the arc of the putter, the club hit the man square in his forehead, with a more powerful upswing that made contact with the bone right above his right eye. Matt could hear the impact of the bone along with the air that seemed to escape from the man's lungs as he was falling backwards to the floor.

Matt decided not to stay around and see if the man was alive or dead, but instead dropped the putter and ran for the front doors. He decided not to wait for the elevator and moved toward the exit door and down the building stairwells. Matt moved at a fast pace, jumping two to three stairs at a time, not knowing if the man was already behind him or was dead from the blow. It didn't matter, he had to get out and he had to find Amanda.

Matt ran out to the office lobby and opened the fire exit door. He wasn't going to wait around for the elevator. He ran down the stairs as fast as he could. He found Amanda waiting in the lobby. She jumped back as the exit door flew open.

When she saw him, she ran to him and hugged him. He hugged her back.

"Are you okay?"

"Yeah," Matt said. "I have the disc."

"They killed the security guard." Amanda said.

Matt looked back at the security desk and saw the guard slumped back against his chair.

Then she asked "Who was up there?"

"I think there was only one man. I think he's still up there."

"Let's get out of here." She said. "I called the police."

Then they heard the sirens.

A minute later there were two cars and four officers. The blue lights of the cars were ricocheting off the glass and steel of the building's lobby. The sirens whirled to a halt. Amanda's call had been about an intruder in an office building. Amanda had added that the man carried a weapon.

The officers exited their cars and drew their weapons. Amanda and Matt ran up to meet the police officers as they approached the building.

"The security guard has been killed," Amanda said.

"I think a man is still in the building, twenty-sixth floor." Matt added.

"How many did you see?" The more senior looking of the police officers asked. One of the other officers was speaking into the radio relaying the information to his dispatcher.

"I just think one." Matt said.

"Why don't you two get in the back of the car and stay there. We'll check it out."

"No, I need to take you up there." Matt said. "I can show you where he was, I think he's injured."

"How did he get injured?" one of the other officers asked.

"I hit him in the head with my boss's putter," Matt said.

The officers gave Matt a "sure you did" kind of look.

"I'll show you where he is." Matt said. "I turned the lights out from the electrical box in the office. The lights are still out."

"Okay, but you have to stay back behind us." The senior officer said.

Matt turned to Amanda and said "Wait here. I'll be right back."

"Matt, are you sure you should do this?" Amanda had a worried look in her face.

"Not at all," Matt said as a retort. "But this time there's five of us."

Rather than climbing the twenty six floors to Matt's office, the police chose the elevator. The ride up was fast. No one spoke. The officers readied their weapons as the soft ping of the elevator doors sounded, like jockeys waiting at their starting gates. The doors opened and Matt quietly stepped back to the corner of the elevator in case the shooting started right away.

But nothing happened.

The officers used their flashlights to find their way to the reception area of the firm. They turned to Matt. The flashlights illuminating his face like a Halloween ghost. "Show us where you saw him," they said.

Matt pointed down the hallway in the direction of Dwight's office and the flashlights turned to lead the way. Matt started thinking that he had probably killed his assailant on the second hit, the one that put him down. But then Matt considered the size of the man and figured that it would have had to have been a lucky hit if it killed him. Matt wasn't feeling guilty about what he had done, if he had actually killed the man. Matt had already convinced himself that the man deserved it.

As they walked further down the hall, Matt moved to the front of the group and led them to the corner in front of Smith's office. There was no body. There was a small pool of blood that glistened under the flood of the multiple flashlights. The lights then followed the trail of dark stains left in the carpet as the man moved to the same stairway exit that Amanda had used to leave the building.

"Let me turn the lights back on," Matt said. He moved by instinct and by following the hallway wall until he found the electrical box to trigger the circuit.

By the time the lights were fully on, the policemen had decided to follow the trail down the stairwell. Matt was instructed to return to the police car and to meet them there. He was escorted down to the lobby by one of the new officers that had arrived on the scene.

"What happened tonight sir?" the young officer asked.

Matt answered carefully. "Someone tried to steal some very valuable information from me."

"They must have wanted it bad," the officer responded

"Enough to kill for," Matt answered.

When Matt exited the elevator into the building lobby there were now at least ten others who had arrived on the scene. He noticed that the security guard had been moved to a gurney and had been covered with a sheet. Two men were photographing the area. Matt made his way through the revolving door and out toward the police car where Amanda had been waiting. She was gone.

CHAPTER 50

Although Matt's story to the police was convoluted, they understood that the man who had killed the security guard and had tried to kill Matt had now taken Amanda. They did not understand what that man had been trying to get from Matt. He told them it had something to do with his father's death, but he did not tell them about the disc. The police put out an APB for the 6'4" Caucasian man with the buzz cut and the injury to his jaw and forehead. He was noted as armed and dangerous. Then they put out a missing persons report on Amanda. They listed it as a possible kidnapping.

Matt was expecting the worse. They had not killed her there. They had only one reason to keep her alive.

Matt knew that if he went to the FBI or the NTSB now they would just kill Amanda. She was only alive to keep Matt honest. He knew they would be in touch with him. But eventually they would plan to kill both of them, just as they had done with Saunders and Tanner. No loose ends, Matt thought.

He was released by the police, although reluctantly, since they warned him that whoever had tried to hurt him at his office might certainly try again. It was already after midnight by the time he was given an escort to his car. After they checked his back seat and trunk along with doing a once over for any car bombs, Matt just got into the car, thanked them again for the help and began his drive home. As he was driving, he couldn't stop thinking that he had put Amanda's life in jeopardy and how responsible he would feel if anything happened to her.

They would contact him, he thought. They would have to.

Without really knowing how he had made it home without causing an accident, Matt drove up his street and up his driveway. Instead of going into the garage, Matt again stopped his car in the driveway. He walked up to his front door. Matt carefully opened the door and made his way through the foyer toward the kitchen. He didn't really believe that they were in the house, but the events of the evening had admittedly made him paranoid.

"Matt."

Matt jumped and turned, it was Linda

"Oh my God, you scared me. I didn't know you'd be here. When did you come home?" His heart was beating out of his chest. Matt was trying to catch his breath between his questions

"Is Sally with you?"

"No," Linda said.

"Are you all right?" she asked, surprised by Matt's reaction.

"You just scared me. You'll understand after I tell you what happened," he added.

"What are you doing here?" his question was somewhat accusatory.

"I couldn't stay away any longer. Sally stayed with my mom. I had to come back."

Matt stepped toward her, they looked at each other, almost as if both of them had changed, but were the same. They embraced.

He held her and looked at her. Then he looked past her.

"Matt, what is happening? What's wrong? You haven't called me, please tell me."

He looked back up into her eyes. It was Linda. He took a deep breath and exhaled.

"So much has happened. I wanted you to be safe, but I'm so glad you're here," he said.

"Matt," she asked, "what has happened? The disc, did you find it?"

"Yes," he said. "I need to tell you everything."

Matt took her hand and they walked to the couch to sit down next to each other.

He would tell her about Amanda, he would tell her everything, but mostly about the fact that she had helped him and now she would die if he didn't help her.

His wife listened, she was strong. But she was scared.

"Matt, what are you going to do?" She asked.

"The first thing is to create a bargaining chip. I need to make a copy of the disc. Then I need to wait until they call me."

Matt walked into his home office, took out a clean disc and began the process of copying the files from Saunders disc.

Just as he was finished, the phone rang. The called id once again said "caller unknown."

Matt picked up the phone.

"Yes," Matt said.

"You have something I want. We have something you want."

The voice was different Matt thought, deeper, older.

"Who is this?" Matt said.

"I think you know Mr. Taggart," the voice said. "You've been doing your homework. But this nonsense stops now! I'll see you at my office noon tomorrow. Bring the disc. Come alone. You call anyone to help you. Ms. Silver dies. Do you understand?"

"Yes I do." Matt said

Then the line went dead.

"What?" Linda said, "what did they say?"

"It's an exchange. The disc for Amanda. At his office. It was Wykert. They want to meet at ADX."

"They'll kill you Matt, just like they did the other men. You'll never get out alive." Linda said. "You have to call the police."

Matt thought for a moment.

"Will you help me?" he asked his wife.

"Of course I will. What do you need me to do?" she asked.

And then he told her.

CHAPTER 51

At nine o'clock the next morning, Linda got into her car and backed out of the garage and drove away, Matt walked alongside watching her. She stopped at the end of the driveway and looked back at Matt. He could see she was crying. She looked away and drove down the street. Matt walked back into the house and gathered his paperwork. He turned off the lights and walked out the front door to his car. It would take him about an hour and a half to reach ADX's offices.

Linda drove directly to the NTBS office, parked in the office garage and walked up to the receptionist. "I'm Linda Taggart. I need to see Director Nickels. It's an emergency."

The lady at the desk picked up the phone and repeated the words to his secretary. The receptionist got out of her chair and said to Linda "please follow me" and guided her back to the Director's office.

Nickels rose from his desk when she walked in. "Mrs. Taggart, how can I help you?"

"It's about the Senator's plane. Matt has discovered a disc."

Nickels looked over to his secretary. "Tracy, will you excuse us please?"

"Certainly, Mr. Nickels." She turned and closed the office door behind her. Nickels led Linda to a seating area in front of his desk. She sat on the couch. He sat in the larger leather chair across from her.

"Now what's this all about?" He asked.

Linda told Nickels what Matt had told her to say, including the kidnapping of Amanda Silver

"Do you know where she is?" He asked.

"Yes. She's being held by Max Wykert at ADX. She's being held in exchange for the disc." Linda said "My husband is going there right now to deliver the disc to Mr. Wykert in exchange for Ms. Silvers' freedom. But they have already killed two men, including your diver, Mr. Tanner. The disc explains why."

"My husband wanted you to call the FBI." she added.

Nickels rose off out of the chair. "Yes. I understand. That would make sense."

He paced back and forth behind his desk. He looked confused. Then Nickels picked up the phone.

"Would you please bring my car around?"

Linda was surprised by Nickels response and suddenly realized that he was not going to call the FBI as Matt had asked.

"You need to call the FBI!" She demanded. "You need to help my husband!" Her voice was shaking as she spoke.

"It's all under control Mrs. Taggart. I promise you that. Please come with me."

He took her by the elbow and escorted her out the back door of his office, down a set of stairs and to his awaiting black town car. He placed her in the back seat and then sat down beside her. The car then turned out of the underground garage and took a left turn.

"Where are you taking me?" Linda demanded to know. Her eyes had started to tear. She was angry. But now she was afraid.

"We are going to join your husband, Mrs. Taggart."

"But why?" Linda asked. And then she realized she knew the answer to her question.

She looked for the driver. The barrier was up between the front seat and the back. She looked at her door. It had been locked. She looked out the window. All she could think about was Sally and Matt.

CHAPTER 52

Matt took the exit off the expressway and carefully followed the street signs that led back to the ADX office building. There was a security guard at the gatehouse and he asked for Matt's name. The guard asked Matt to drive to the administration building and wait to be met there.

Matt did as he was told. He parked his car and took his briefcase from the back seat of his car and walked into the building where he was met by another guard. He was asked to sit down in a waiting area. While Matt sat down in the row of chairs in the reception area the guard opened a door at the end of the hall and closed the door behind him. Matt noticed the security camera in the corner of the reception area. He tried not to look up at it while it turned toward him. He was wondering if Amanda could see that he was there. He knew that Wykert would be watching.

A moment later the door down the hall opened again and the guard returned to escort Matt into the building.

"This way," was all the man said. His eyes were focused on Matt, aware, but not threatened.

"You work for Wykert?" Matt said. The young guard did not provide a response.

The man walked beside Matt and directed him to the last office on his left. It was there that he entered the cavernous office of Max Wykert.

As he walked into the office he confronted the "Universal Soldier" he had met the night before. His eye was bandaged, his forehead swollen.

"Turn around," the man said.

"What?" Matt replied.

"I want to see Ms. Silver," Matt said.

"Listen asshole," the large man said. "If I had my way, I'd just break you in two right here. You got lucky last night. You won't again. But right now, I just need to make sure you're not carrying. So turn around. It can be easy or hard, your choice."

Matt turned around and in an instant the man had pushed Matt up against the wall hard, his elbow pushing against Matt's neck as he used his other hand to check Matt's belt and back. Then he released Matt.

"Where is she?" Matt asked again. The soldier did not respond.

"Let me see the briefcase," the man said.

Matt handed the man the leather briefcase.

"You open it." he said.

Matt knelt down on one knee and moved the tumblers for the combination. The briefcase clicked open. The man went through the papers, found nothing that could be used as a weapon and said "close it."

He then turned and spoke to the security camera in the corner of the room. "All clear," the man spoke aloud.

Suddenly a door in the back corner of the large office opened and an older, well-dressed man emerged. He was bald, had round spectacle-type glasses and looked all the part of eighty in the wrinkles of his face and his hands. His eyes were dark, yet glassy in appearance.

"Welcome Mr. Taggart," the man said as he approached Matt. His voice was strong and clear. He was Matt's height, maybe an inch or two taller, but bowed in the neck making him appear shorter. The man held out his hand. Matt shook it. It did not cross his mind to reject his offer. "You have been an unexpected obstacle in my plan," Mr. Taggart. "But your interference ends now. Mr. Taylor, bring in Ms. Silver please."

The soldier exited for just a moment and then brought in Amanda, her face bruised, her clothes torn.

"Ah, the lovely Ms. Silver. Quite a fighter, but alas, no match for Mr. Taylor here."

"Did you enjoy your stay here Ms. Silver?" Wykert was clearly sarcastic in his tone.

"Matt, I'm so sorry," was all Amanda said.

"Sit please, both of you, we will discuss our plans in just a moment, but we await another visitor." Wykert said.

"Who?" Matt asked.

"But of course, Director Nickels and your lovely wife." Wykert calmly responded.

Matt spoke under his breath. "If you touch her, I will kill you," Matt said.

"You are in no position to threaten anyone Mr. Taggart." Wykert quickly answered, the volume of his voice increasing.

"I assume Mr. Taggart, that you brought what I requested." Wykert was now staring at Matt. "I know now that you will give it to me, if not for your girlfriend, then certainly for your wife, the mother of your young child."

Matt returned the stare.

Wykert stood. "I'll be back in a few moments. Mr. Taylor will keep you company while you wait."

"Oh Matt, I'm so sorry, not Linda too," Amanda turned to him.

"It's my fault. I sent her to get help from Director Nickels, to call the FBI." Matt answered.

"But I told you that Nickels didn't believe me when I told him that the report must have been wrong. Even after Tanner's murder, he still didn't believe me," she reminded him.

"But I thought he would help us if Linda went to him." Matt explained.

"I'm sorry about all of this Matt." Amanda said.

"It's not your fault Amanda. It's Wykert." Matt offered. "He'll pay for this."

They sat there. Their heads down. They looked lost, as if they knew they had been defeated by Wykert. The soldier watching them enjoyed their misery.

About twenty minutes later Nickels walked into the room and pulled along Linda. Matt ran to her and she hugged him. She was crying.

"Honey I'm so sorry," Matt said.

"Nickels is behind it too," she said. "He pushed the suicide finding. He told me."

"I know," Matt said. "Now, I know."

Linda turned and surveyed the room. She saw Amanda.

"Amanda?" Linda asked.

"Yes," Amanda replied.

Matt interrupted.

"Amanda, this is my wife Linda."

"I'm sorry Ms. Taggart, for everything."

"No, I understand. It's okay. Thank you for helping Matt. Are you okay?"

"Yes. It looks worse then it is. It's my fault. I wouldn't go without a fight."

Just then the door opened again and Max Wykert entered the room.

"So, has everyone gotten reacquainted?"

"Mrs. Taggart I presume, so nice to meet you. I see that you have met Ms. Silver. The both of you are so lovely. So hard to pick Mr. Taggart? Having your cake and eating it too?"

"Why did you kill my father?" Matt stepped forward only to be blocked by Taylor.

"So direct Mr. Lawyer. Well, I assume you deserve an answer, at least after what you've been through and what you're going to go through."

Matt looked back at Linda, Linda at Amanda.

"So here's the story. Your father, as magnanimous a man he was to those less fortunate then he, never understood my need to sell this plane. He stopped me for years with his budget concerns. It had to stop. The idea was simple really, pre-program a flight recorder. After the plane crashes substitute the one with the data that shows it to be an accident rather then foul play. In this case, I thought the suicide was a nice touch."

"You're crazy," Matt said.

"Maybe so, young Taggart, but don't you agree, creative?"

Mr. Saunders, the engineer from Bluestone was given the task to create the replacement recorder, but without understanding its purpose or intent, simply as an engineering exercise. He did what he was told. It appears however, that he was smarter then we anticipated and was able to piece together the facts of your father's crash and the information he inputted into the recorder. That curiosity cost him his life, did it not?"

Wykert was now pacing back and forth in the room, almost bouncy from his storytelling.

"But he made a copy of the information, didn't he Mr. Taggart. Quite an insurance policy, or so he thought. Quite a disappointment to rid ourselves of him and Mr. Tanner, our qualified diver. But for a better cause . . . . national security . . . 100 fighter planes."

Then Amanda spoke up. "I understand the switch on the box, but how did the plane crash? What did you do to Senator Taggart?"

"Ah, the investigator seeks the answer to her errors. What did you miss? That's what you're asking, isn't it Ms. Silver? What was your mistake?"

Amanda did not answer. She did not look up.

"Again, simple my dear, the plane crash itself was easy. An operative of ours placed a small explosive charge near the pilot's window that smashed the window at 17,000 feet. Your father would have lost consciousness immediately, therefore, no call for help." Wykert went on with his story, "the plane had no auto pilot so, without a conscious pilot, it was a deadstick dive. But we couldn't simply make it appear as if he crashed. No, I wanted something more and I had my engineers create the pre-recorded flight recorder. So when Mr. Nickels' diver retrieved the real box, he simply switched it for the pre-recorded one. Voila, the suicide."

"Certainly, Mr. Nickels earned his pay by pushing his staff to reach the conclusion they did and cease any further investigation. They are all so busy there, aren't they Leonard?"

Nickels looked up and then away. He had been paid well for the coverup for the accident. He never thought it would have led to the murders and now this kidnapping.

"So there you have it. Enough!" Wykert said. "Now, Mr. Taggart, give me the disc."

"Let Linda and Amanda go first. That was our deal," Matt said.

"Deal? Deal? The budget vote is days away. No one is going anywhere. Give me the disc." Wykert demanded.

"Give it to me Mr. Taggart or Mr. Taylor will be required to finish what he started last night." Wykert threatened.

The large man approached Matt and Matt stood up.

"You greedy son of a bitch," Matt lunged at Wykert.

Taylor pushed him down.

"Mr. Taylor, please help Mr. Taggart give me the disc."

As Taylor approached, Amanda stood up. Linda did too.

Taylor turned toward the woman as they stood and, with one eye covered with the bandage, he had to turn his head almost to the other side to see them clearly. As he spoke the words, "this will be my pleasure" Matt had time to reach for the briefcase that had sat next to his chair. He stood up and swung the briefcase across the side of Taylor's head. He didn't see it coming. It hit him hard, but not hard enough. He stumbled.

As he regained his footing, Amanda kicked him in the groin. He went down to one knee.

"Bitch!" He was angry.

It was during this chaos that Matt finally heard the sirens that he had been waiting for. Wykert heard them too.

Matt then unloaded one of the chairs across Taylor's back. The man fell flat.

Nickels led Wykert out of the back door of the office.

The young guard entered from the front door.

"Stop!" The young guard said. He reached for his sidearm and pulled the gun from the holster.

"Shoot them," Taylor said.

The sirens got louder and the young guard heard them. He held the gun pointed first at Matt, then Amanda, then Linda.

"Shoot them," Taylor ordered again.

The young guard remained steady, but refused to fire. Taylor rose and while the gun was pointed at the three others, followed Wykert and Nickels out the rear door.

CHAPTER 53

Minutes passed as Matt tried to explain to the young soldier what was happening. But the guard chose to wait for the approaching sirens to figure out if their story was true. He did not believe that Max Wykert was a murderer.

The delay gave Wykert, Nickels and Taylor the opportunity to escape. When the FBI entered the room, the soldier dropped his weapon. He was immediately taken down to the floor and handcuffed.

"Agent Jonas, you are a sight for sore eyes," Matt said

"Nice to see you too, Matt. Your call came out of the blue," the agent responded.

"Wykert's getting away," Matt said. "They went out the back door."

Some of the FBI agents ran past Matt following Wykert and his accomplices.

"Matt, what's going on?" both Linda and Amanda said simultaneously.

"Back up plan. Someone I knew I could trust." Matt answered.

"What about Nickels?" Linda said with a confused look.

"He either would have called the FBI too or he was behind it." Matt answered.

"Amanda, you led me to figure that out. When you told me Nickels didn't believe you, even after Tanner was killed. Either he was involved or too stupid to understand."

A moment or so later Jonas' radio sounded.

"They're gone, sir."

"How did they get away?" Jonas asked.

"It looks like there's a back road behind the office. They must have had a car," the voice said.

"It's a black town car. He had a driver." Linda said.

Jonas quickly alerted his men to put an APB out on the car and called in for air assistance.

"Where could they go?" Matt asked.

"They know their cover is blown. They're going to try to leave." Amanda answered.

"I agree," Jonas said. "Any idea where they could go?" Jonas asked.

"Did you know that Wykert was a pilot?" Matt offered to the FBI agent.

"What kind of pilot?" Jonas responded.

"I'm not sure, but when I was doing research on ADX, I think Wykert still has his pilot license and a plane," Matt said.

The agent then turned to another agent and barked, "find out right now if he has a plane and where it's hangered."

"Yes, sir," the younger agent responded.

"Not bad Matt," Amanda said. "Smart thinking to call the FBI."

"You could have told me," his wife said in an angry tone.

"I didn't know, but it was one way to figure it out."

"What now?" Amanda said.

"We have to find Wykert." Matt said, "and we have to let the true story out."

"Matt, do you still have the disc?" his wife asked.

"Yes, and this will help too," Matt said. He opened his briefcase, pulled down a zippered compartment and removed a small tape recorder. Matt pointed to the small microphone in the handle of the case.

"Nothing better then a taped confession." Matt laughed with pride.

Agent Jonas approached them. "All right, we've got the bulletin out and we're contacting local airports for information about any planes registered to ADX or Wykert. I think its time to take you all home."

"Sounds good to me," Matt said.

As they were climbing into the sedan, Jonas got a call on his walkie talkie.

"We found it sir. About twenty miles from here. It's a regional airport. Wykert has a twin prop plane."

Jonas looked at Matt. He could tell from his expression that he wanted to be there when Wykert was arrested. "Let's go," Jonas said.

CHAPTER 54

Nickels' driver who was oblivious to what had transpired in the directors office or at ADX followed the new instructions to follow the dirt road back to the main road and head for the airport.

Taylor sat in the front passenger seat and Wykert and Nickels sat in the rear.

Wykert turned to Nickels in the sedan and said "sloppy work Leonard."

"I did everything you asked Max." Nickels responded in his defense.

"But you did it poorly. Loose ends. Unforgiveable." Wykert answered curtly.

"Max, we can still put a cover on this." Nickels spoke, making a statement but offering it as a hopeful suggestion.

"No, Leonard. We can't." Wykert's tone was now quiet, resolved.

"Mr. Taylor," Wykert called to the front passenger, "your assistance please."

Before Leonard Nickels knew what had happened, the man turned and produced a gun. Taylor was finishing his final turns to the silencer as he attached it to the weapon. Nickels stared at the shiny black object as if he was curious to understand its shape and its meaning. But then he realized what was happening. He turned toward Max to beg for his life. But the pop that followed stopped the words from escaping his voicebox. Instead a sound of air escaped his lungs from the small hole now located in his chest.

Leonard Nickels felt a warm, gel like substance against his chest. He reached his hand up to touch his shirt, then pulled his hand away and saw the blood. He leaned back and knew that he was going to die.

The driver saw Taylor turn and heard the same popping sound that found Nickels' heart. He instinctively turned the car off the road to see what had happened. As he braked Taylor then turned the gun on him. The man reacted by opening the car door to attempt a quick exit and escape, knowing that to stay there would only result in a similar fate to what had happened to his boss. No words were spoken, he knew it wouldn't matter. He did not need to request permission to run, he just needed to do it. But as he opened the door, Taylor also acted instinctively, raising the gun to the man's back. Taylor felt no hesitancy as he pulled the trigger and shot him. The force of the shot urged the driver's body the remaining way out of the vehicle, where it simply dropped to the ground.

Taylor then opened his door, exited the passenger seat, made his way around to the other side of the car. He opened the back door to remove Nickel's body from the car. He took both arms and pulled him from the back seat. Max Wykert leaned back in his seat and lit his cigar. Taylor only dragged the body a few feet and left it on the side of the road. He had no concern about trying to hide the body. In fact, leaving the body that way displayed the message. They would kill anyone who got in their way. Taylor returned to the car, used his foot to kick the driver's body away from the front door and took his place to drive the rest of the way.

As the car wheels spun away from the roadside, the gravel spit back at the two bodies laying on the roadside. Boss and employee lay one next to the other, both in dark blue suits, white shirts, ties. One body was indistinguishable from the other. Nickels' power and wealth had not protected him from the same fate which had befallen his driver. Both died the same way. One punished for his criminal act, one having only been at the wrong place at the wrong time.

As they entered the airport property where Wykert stored his plane, Wykert flashed the elderly security guard his property pass and Taylor drove the vehicle down the road to where the plane was parked. It had already been pre-fueled. Wykert had made that call as they left ADX. Taylor parked the vehicle and both men approached the plane. Wykert turned to Taylor and gave him instructions to release the wing tethers and the wheel blocks. Wykert climbed the stairs up to the plane and took his seat as the pilot. He knew that the police and FBI would not be far behind them. He would not be filing a flight plan today.

He never hid the fact from anyone that he was a pilot and that he had a plane. He had not planned for an escape by air. He actually had never assumed that his would happen, that he would be running from the law. But he was not concerned. He had money in banks overseas. He had his connections, favors to be returned, men that could be bought. He would get away.

Taylor climbed into the airplane, turned and pulled up the stairs. He took the seat next to Wykert. The engine turned over and Wykert began moving the plane toward the runway about 150 yards away.

When they reached the airport, Jonas showed his badge to the security guard and asked the question. The answer came in the form of an outstretched arm pointing to the small plane that was now moving away from the nearby hanger and toward the runway.

"That's him," Matt said, "there's his plane"

Jonas pressed the accelerator and drove straight, moving the car ahead of the plane about 50 feet. Jonas stopped the car and got out. His weapon was drawn and he moved his arms back and forth with his badge. He was trying to signal the pilot to stop the plane.

Matt, Linda and Amanda exited from the car and stood to watch as the agent walked closer to the plane. He continued to gesture to the pilot to shut down the engine. There was no response. Wykert stayed in the cockpit, looked directly at the agent and then turned the plane in the other direction toward a larger area of the tarmac.

Jonas turned back toward the car and used his radio to notify the other agents that were arriving at the airport that the plane was moving to the runway.

"You can't let him get away!" Matt yelled at him over the sound of the plane's engine, "you have to do something."

"We have to wait for back up," Jonas answered.

Matt decided not to wait. He opened the driver's door and, with keys still in the ignition, started the car and headed straight for the plane. Jonas, Amanda and Linda all stood back yelling at Matt to stop.

Once Matt caught up with the plane he drove alongside it as it taxied. He attempted to steer the plane off the runway. The plane did not move off its course.

It was then that Matt decided to try to block the plane. It only had another forty feet or so before it could start its acceleration for takeoff. Matt moved the car directly in front of the plane's left wing. This time Wykert blinked and moved the plane first to the right and then back to the left. Matt moved further into the area of the left wheel base and Wykert continued to adjust the plane to avoid possible damage. If the plane hit the car or vice versa, the plane would probably not be able to take off. Suddenly, the window on the pilot's side of the plane slide opened, and the barrel of a gun appeared, firing at the car. The passenger window in Matt's car smashed apart with the gunshot and Matt turned the car away from the gunfire.

The plane didn't stop. Wykert gunned the engine and moved forward. After 100 feet and at seventy to eighty miles an hour the plane kept going. Matt decided the only thing he could do was to get ahead of the plane and block the runway with his car. Matt stepped deep on the gas pedal and he pulled ahead of the plane to the middle of the runway. He watched as the plane moved toward him, like a runaway train barreling through a car crossing an intersection. The plane continued to move faster although it had nowhere to go. It was a foolish game of chicken since Matt realized that he had no time to get out of the car, but Wykert must have also realized that he could not hit and car and still fly the plane. At the last minute, Wykert swerved to avoid the car and Matt watched at the right wing passed over the car, clipping the roof. The car bounced, shuddered and fell back to its wheels. The plane however, had lost its balance and turned off the runway.

The plane continued, with its engine still engaged at full throttle, and in the direction of the airport maintenance area. Matt opened the car door and watched as the plane bounced along the grassy route, slowing some, but not enough to prevent its collision with the first of three small buildings. The resulting impact engaged the fuel tank of the plane and the flames started before the plane hit the third of the buildings which contained flammable materials.

The explosion was bright and large and loud. Matt could feel the heat of the flames even though he was over a football field away from where the plane had exploded. Matt felt certain that Wykert and Taylor had remained in the plane.

As Matt watched the plane burn, two cars pulled up beside Matt. Linda, Amanda and agent Jonas emerged from the cars. Linda ran to Matt.

"Are you all right?" she asked, as she buried him in her arms.

"I'm fine," Matt said, still mesmerized by the flames.

"Matt, you're one crazy son of a bitch." Jonas said.

"You're probably right," Matt answered. "But those are the guys who killed my father."

The fire burned for a while before the fire crews could reach the plane, and longer for the metal to cool before the investigators could identify that they had found the remains of two bodies, otherwise unidentifiable due to the damage caused by the heat and the flames.

CHAPTER 55

Jonas drove Matt, Linda and Amanda back to D.C. and directly to FBI headquarters to begin the debriefing. Along the way, the reports came in concerning the location of the bodies of Leonard Nickels and his driver.

During the debriefing, Matt explained to the agent in charge that he needed to tell his family what had happened before they saw it on television. They discussed it a minute, but Matt was adamant that they find out from him. He left the room to make the call.

He pulled out his cell phone and dialed her number.

"Hello," the voice was quiet.

"Mom," it's Matt.

"Matt, what's wrong, is everything okay?" Her voice sounded scared.

"I have some news about Dad," he said.

"What honey, what news?" she asked.

"Mom, Dad's plane was sabotaged. He didn't kill himself." As he said the words himself, he realized the significance of what he was saying.

The line was silent. She was still listening, but was clearly still taking in what he had said.

"Not suicide?" She sounded confused.

"No Mom . . . he was murdered."

She was starting to realize what he was saying to her. "He was murdered? By who?"

"It was a company that wanted a government contract that Dad was opposed to. It was all politics Mom."

"The plane? What about the plane?" she asked again.

"They rigged the plane to crash. It wasn't Dad. It was them. They wanted him out of the way"

"They were caught? Are they in jail?" she asked.

"They're dead Mom. They were killed trying to escape."

Matt decided any more would be too much. "Mom, I'm going to come see you this weekend. I'll explain everything, okay?"

"Okay. But when will people learn that your Dad did not kill himself."

"Soon Mom, very soon." Matt replied.

"Thank you Matt. Thank you. That's such good news. He was a good man. He should not have died."

"No Mom, he shouldn't have died. But now it's all over."

"Does Jenny or Roger know?" she asked.

"Not yet, I'll call them too. Okay?"

"Okay." She said.

Matt said "Goodbye Mom, I'll call you tomorrow okay?"

Matt hit the end button of the phone.

Although the media had gotten wind of the APB for Wykert and the scene at the Municipal Airport, Matt decided that his mother was right. People had to know what happened. He went through the list of names on his cell phone. "I'm sure I put it in here," Matt said to himself. He found what he was looking for and he hit "dial" on the phone.

A voice answered. "Hello, Howard Goldman."

Matt started. "Howard, its Matthew Taggart."

"Matt? How are you?" Goldman asked.

"Great," Matt said. "I have something for you to listen to," and Matt pulled the tape recorder from his jacket pocket.

"Are you ready?" Matt said with a smile.

It was close to 9:00 at night before Matt and Linda had made it home after the debriefing. He had called Roger on his cell phone on the ride home. He called Jenny from his house.

While he was talking to Jenny on the phone, Linda walked into the den holding two glasses of red wine. She sat on the couch next to Matt and handed him his glass.

"Jenny. I'll call you tomorrow." Matt said. "Yeah, <u>The Washington Post</u>," he added.

"Bye" Matt said. He wanted the conversation to end. Linda had put her arm around his shoulder and was rubbing her hands through his hair.

He was still on the phone as Linda kissed him on the ear and then his neck.

"Sis, I really have to go," Matt said, "Linda needs me. Bye" Matt hung up the phone.

Matt turned to Linda.

"Yes, I really do need you." She repeated

She leaned forward and kissed him gently on the mouth.

"I love you," she said.

He looked back at her. He kissed her once and then pulled her toward him. He held her tight. "I love you too," Matt said.

CHAPTER 56

It had been a quick deadline for Goldman since the story appeared the very next morning as the front page headline, entitled "Senator's Death a Murder, Not Suicide." Goldman's story included Matt's discovery of the disc, the scene at Wykert's office and the crash at the airport. The story included a copy of Wykert's taped confession. Matt had left out the part about using the car to block the plane. Goldman had learned about that stunt from talking with Amanda.

By eight o'clock in the morning, after the story hit the wires, the Taggart family was being bombarded by calls for interviews from television stations and reporters. Katy Couric had left a personal message for Matt at the house to call her to see if he could appear on the Today Show.

Matt and Linda were outside in the backyard blowing bubbles with Sally.

Over the next few days, Matt learned from Amanda that the NTSB and the FBI had reinspected the plane with their forensic team and discovered the location of the detonation that had demolished the windshield. As Wykert had described, the detonation had cracked the windshield of the plane to create cabin depressurization which would have caused his father to pass out from the altitude. Without a conscious pilot, the plane was certain to crash, which it did. But with the data recorder showing all systems operative except for the apparent intentional change in flight altitude, the N.T.S.B. had no reason to investigate any other cause for the downed plane. Even when the N.T.S.B retrieved the plane, Amanda explained, they would not have discovered the damage to the cabin from the small explosion due to the condition of the plane after the crash and the addition of the salt water to the systems. However, Nickels had issued a report on the findings from the flight recorder and, under his direction, the investigation had been a quick one. Amanda began to accept the fact that even if she had discovered some issue with the plane, Nickels would have likely quashed the investigation.

It had been a sham. All of it. The perfect plan. Kill off a senator, pin the crash on a suicide, no foul play investigated. They just needed the guy to create a flight recorder with the information they wanted and arrange to switch the boxes at the crash site. Apparently, Saunders was the guy who ignorantly designed the system and Tanner was the one paid to make the switch. Nickels was the one who had watched over all of it.

After the story broke, the Senate Appropriations Committee cancelled their budget vote, and once again the F-20 would remain unbuilt. The rumor on the Hill was that the President would be forced to appoint a Special Prosecutor to investigate the ADX contract, the Pentagon's involvement in the project, and the N.T.S.B. negligence in allowing the tampering of evidence. The chain of custody had been broken.

Within two weeks the F.B.I. investigation was in full swing and senate hearings were scheduled to address the process of approving defense contracts. The night before he was to appear before the Senate subcommittee to testify, Colonel Brier was found dead in his home from a single gunshot wound. The autopsy said it was self inflicted from the gun found next to him on the floor. Matt later learned, from a follow up story written by Howard Goldman, that over the years ADX had greased the skids to the Pentagon by paying Colonel Brier, whose bank accounts under his children's names evidenced payments of over four hundred and fifty thousand dollars.

Matt couldn't help but be suspicious about Brier's death when he read about it. He didn't believe suicide results anymore. He simply pictured Colonel Brier slouched over his desk. The news reports didn't say anything about it, but Matt envisioned him all dressed in his formal uniform, kind of like that officer who killed himself in <u>A Few Good Men</u>. Maybe it was the lack of honor he had shown by selling out, the guilt of being involved in so many deaths, or simply the cowardice of what he would have to face in front of him. To Matt it didn't matter. The man deserved what he got, whether it was from his own hand or from someone else's.

There had been also some turmoil at the N.T.S.B. The agency itself really had done nothing wrong. It was Nickels and Tanner. Both of whom were well paid well for their acts and then paid the ultimate price. Amanda Silver had offered her resignation, but it was refused by the acting director. In fact, it was his recommendation that she be honored for her work and heroism. Each time that Matt and Amanda spoke about what was happening at the NTSB, their conversations were stilted. Both Matt and Amanda knew that what they felt toward each other was borne from the intensity of their experience together. Life and death. But it was over. He had Linda. There was no changing that.

The last time he spoke to Amanda was after Brier had been found dead. She told him that she was leaving town to investigate a plane crash that had happened in Greece. The President had offered his top people to assist the Greek government in their investigation of the accident. Two hundred had died. Twenty-four of them American tourists. She would be gone for a few months. She said she would call him when she got back to town. Matt knew that she would not call him and that he likely would not see her again. It was better that way. For both of them.

CHAPTER 57

It was a beautiful Monday morning in Washington. When he exited the elevator on the twenty-sixth floor of his building, he stopped to look above the glass doors at the sign that said Olimeyer, Barkley & Smith. Today, Matt wasn't dressed in a blue suit like the other lawyers. He was wearing jeans and a white golf shirt with running shoes. He said "good morning" to Laurie the receptionist and made his way down the hall to his office. As he passed by the other offices, he looked in and glanced at the attorneys and paralegals working, many of them on the phone, most looking down at documents. He walked by Dwight Smith's office, noticing that the blood stained carpet had been replaced, and walked the remaining distance to his office door, which was closed. His name plate had already been removed.

"Good morning, Matt," Janine said. "How are you?"

"Great. Never felt better." Matt then opened the door to his office and walked to his office where a single box of personal items had been collected, wrapped and placed. "Thanks for doing this, Janine."

"You're welcome. You didn't have too much."

The box contained the photos of Linda and Sally, the small trophy for a scramble golf tournament he had been in, and his diplomas, desk clock, calculator, and some office junk.

"We'll miss you," Janine said.

"Thanks. I appreciate everything you've done for me."

"I wish I could have done more. You're a good one, Matt."

"Thanks. I'll keep in touch. Someone has to explain how to turn on my computer."

"I just have one more thing to do," Matt said to himself.

Matt opened his briefcase and took out the single sheet of paper.

He walked up the stairway to the Jamison war room where the documents had been organized in anticipation of Davidson's document production, to be done later in the week. The motion to compel had been granted. The motion for reconsideration had been denied. The interlocutory appeal had also been denied. Davidson would have his chance to review the culled documents.

Matt took the single sheet, opened up a box and dropped the paper inside. Matt realized it didn't matter which box he put it in. It would be found, just the same. Matt closed the box, walked out the door and turned off the light.

When he returned to his office, he picked up the box of his photographs and made his way down the hallway, back toward the reception area. He noticed a lot of people looking at him, but they said nothing more than a few "goodbyes" and a few "good lucks." When he reached the elevator lobby, the elevator door opened, and Tom Barkley walked out. He had a surprised look on his face, which simply said to Matt that Tom had wished he hadn't run into him.

"Best of luck to you, Matt," Barkley said.

"Thanks, Tom."

Barkley reached out with his hand and Matt took it, their hands shaking firmly, each looking at the other. "The door is always open for you son," Barkley said.

"Thank you, Tom," Matt responded, and then he continued to the elevator and pressed "L."

Matt thought as the elevator made its way down to the lobby that when Davidson finds the copy of the letter from Dwight Smith to Dr. Charles Rosen about the confidentiality order that Davidson will be smart enough to ask the next series of questions which would hopefully lead him to Cleveland. As for Matt, he properly allowed this letter to "remain" in the file. It was not privileged. It was a letter to an unrelated third party. It was Dwight and Jamison who will have to answer about what they were hiding when they silenced Dr. Rosen. Hopefully, for Ms. Forslin and the others like her, the truth would come out.

Dwight would likely know that it was Matt who put the letter back in the file. But now it didn't matter. It wasn't malpractice and it wasn't an ethical breach. Lawyers can only argue the facts they are given, they can't, or at least shouldn't, change the facts to suit their case. At least that was Matt's theory.

As Matt drove his car out of the building garage, he made his way across the G.W. Bridge into Arlington. After about a two minute drive past the Arlington Metro Station, he pulled up at a small two story townhouse office building and looked at the sign on the building which read, "Matthew J. Taggart, P.C., Attorney at Law." He thought to himself that his dad would have liked the sign. He also thought that his father would have liked his first case. It was a wrongful death case. Matt thought he had a pretty good chance at a strong verdict. The case would be styled, *The Estate of Jason Taggart v. ADX Aeronautics and The United States of America.*

ABOUT THE AUTHOR

After almost 25 years of practicing law, Scott I. Zucker has joined the ranks of other seasoned lawyers who have turned their legal writing skills into the world of fiction writing. In his first book Chain of Custody, Scott has entered the stage of political espionage and criminal investigation.

Scott is a partner in a boutique law firm in Atlanta, Georgia where he specializes in commercial litigation representing companies throughout the country. He is a graduate of Washington University in St. Louis and the George Washington University School of Law. He is married with two children.